Other books by

PEG KEHRET

RUNAWAY TWIN

RUNAWAY — TWIN

WITHDRAWN

Peg Kehret

Dutton Children's Books

DUTTON CHILDREN'S BOOKS

A division of Penguin Young Readers Group

Published by the Penguin Group

Penguin Group (USA) Inc., 375 Hudson Street, New York, New York 10014, U.S.A.
Penguin Group (Canada), 90 Eglinton Avenue East, Suite 700, Toronto, Ontario, M4P 2Y3 Canada
(a division of Pearson Penguin Canada Inc.) | Penguin Books Ltd, 80 Strand, London WC2R 0RL,
England | Penguin Ireland, 25 St Stephen's Green, Dublin 2, Ireland (a division of Penguin Books
Ltd) | Penguin Group (Australia), 250 Camberwell Road, Camberwell, Victoria 3124, Australia
(a division of Pearson Australia Group Pty Ltd) | Penguin Books India Pvt Ltd, 11 Community
Centre, Panchsheel Park, New Delhi - 110 017, India | Penguin Group (NZ), 67 Apollo Drive,
Rosedale, North Shore 0632, New Zealand (a division of Pearson New Zealand Ltd.) | Penguin
Books (South Africa) (Pty) Ltd, 24 Sturdee Avenue, Rosebank, Johannesburg 2196, South Africa
Penguin Books Ltd, Registered Offices: 80 Strand, London WC2R 0RL, England

Library of Congress Cataloging-in-Publication Data

Kehret, Peg.
Runaway twin / by Peg Kehret.—1st ed.   p. cm.
Summary: Thirteen-year-old Sunny, accompanied by a stray dog, takes advantage of
a windfall to travel from her Nebraska foster home to Enumclaw, Washington,
to find the twin sister from whom she was separated at age three.
ISBN 978-0-525-42177-1
[1. Foster home care—Fiction. 2. Voyages and travels—Fiction. 3. Dogs—Fiction.
4. Runaways—Fiction. 5. Twins—Fiction. 6. Sisters—Fiction.] I. Title.
PZ7.K2518Run 2009   [Fic]—dc22   2008048974

Published in the United States by Dutton Children's Books,
a division of Penguin Young Readers Group
345 Hudson Street, New York, New York 10014
www.penguin.com/youngreaders

DESIGNED BY ABBY KUPERSTOCK

Printed in USA | First Edition
1 3 5 7 9 10 8 6 4 2

For Jenny Moller and Jerry Lindsey,
who enrich my life in countless ways

ACKNOWLEDGMENTS

The character of Snickers is based on a real dog who was the cherished companion of Julie Carlton. Julie won the chance to memorialize Snickers in a book when she was the high bidder at The Dog Bowl, an auction benefiting Pasado's Safe Haven. Thank you, Julie, for your generous bid, which helped Pasado's care for their many rescued animals.

If it were not for Casey Karp, I would be a bald woman. Casey solves all my computer problems, thereby saving me from tearing my hair out.

My first proofreader for this book was Brett Konen, who gave me numerous helpful suggestions. She's an astute editor and a terrific granddaughter!

My wonderful pet-sitter, Karrie Kamcheff, enables me to travel without worrying about my furry friends.

Thanks, as always, to Rosanne Lauer and the rest of the talented group at Dutton Children's Books.

RUNAWAY TWIN

1

Most people who have a life-changing experience survive a terrible injury or disease. My life was transformed by a craving for Twinkies.

When I woke up on the first day of summer vacation, I yearned for something sweet, so I decided to celebrate the end of school by eating Twinkies for breakfast. I knew better than to suggest this to my foster mom, Rita, who is a total health-food freak. Rita thinks the perfect breakfast is raw carrots dipped in unsweetened yogurt. For an extra treat, she sprinkles a little flaxseed on the yogurt. Yum-yum.

I dressed, and pulled my hair into a ponytail. I heard

Rita's shower running, so I left a note on the counter. "Rita: I'm going for a walk. Sunny."

Since Rita is always urging me to exercise, I knew that going for a walk would be okay with her. She didn't need to know I was walking to the store to buy Twinkies.

Wouldn't you think the Nebraska Department of Human Social Services (HSS, known as Hiss) would try to match a kid's background with the lifestyle of the foster family she's placed with? In my opinion it is cruel and unusual punishment to put a thirteen-year-old girl who was raised on junk food into a home that serves tofu and cauliflower.

It's hard enough to adjust to a new school and a different neighborhood, often a new town, every few months. It would be comforting to at least get some Snickers bars once in a while, or a big plate of nachos. Instead, I live with Rita, who thinks if she feeds me enough healthy food I will learn to like it. So far this strategy hasn't worked.

Rita remains optimistic, though. She also hopes I'll write about my summer activities because the school gives extra credit to any student who turns in an essay, story, or poem on the first day of school in September. This year's topic is "What I Did This Summer." How boring! Eating Twinkies for breakfast will probably be the highlight of my summer, and it would be hard to make an essay out of that.

Two blocks from Rita's house, I left the sidewalk, cut diagonally across an empty lot, and took the trail. It isn't an official trail yet, although it will be someday when the county parks department gets enough money to maintain it. For now, it's a well-worn path that runs parallel to Silver Creek.

I have to watch where I walk because the trail is full of potholes created by the dirt bikes and quads that roar along it while thick curtains of dust drift down behind them. The morning sun warmed my shoulders as I relished the summer that stretched ahead with no homework and no tests. Rita had suggested summer school as a way to improve my grade point average, but she backed down when I threatened to run away again.

I had run away from my last two foster homes, and Rita was determined not to let it happen on her watch. She prided herself on winning over even the most uncooperative foster kids. That's why she'd agreed to take me.

I'm not a bad girl. I don't do drugs or shoplift or anything like that, but I don't do much schoolwork, either.

Why bother when I'll be in a different school by the end of the term anyway? Why participate in sports or try to make friends when I always leave so soon?

As for running away, I don't really want to leave Rita. I ran away before because Hiss put me in unbearable foster homes. In one, the man of the house believed he was Boss of the World. He had to have complete control of everyone, even his wife. He kept track of how long it took his kids to walk home from school, and punished them if they dawdled or stood on the corner talking with friends. He monitored how much toilet paper we used.

I left after he wouldn't let me have dinner because I had held the refrigerator door open too long while I looked for the mustard. It turned out I couldn't find it because the mustard had been used up the last time they had hot dogs, but that didn't matter. I still had to go to bed hungry. How was I supposed to know they needed a new bottle of mustard?

I sneaked out in the night and started walking. I didn't know where I was going, and I didn't care. Any place would be better than staying another day, with the Boss of the World. Hiss found me the next day but when I told the caseworker why I ran away, she said I didn't have to go back. I think the toilet paper part got to her.

Unfortunately, I went from the Boss of the World to living with She Who Hates Anything Pretty. She-Who didn't let me wear makeup, even if I had a zit to cover up. She-Who wouldn't let me curl my hair, which is straight as a shelf.

"If God had wanted you to have curly hair," she said, "you would have been born with it."

"Then why did God allow the invention of the curling iron?" I asked. I've noticed that people who claim to know what God wants always manage to have His opinion be the same as theirs.

She insisted I wear clothes that were a size too large and clunky, old-lady shoes. Small wonder I didn't make any new friends at school. I looked like an eighty-year-old weirdo.

After I ran away from She-Who, I was placed with Rita. It is my seventh foster home. Some were okay. The Boss of the World and She Who Hates Anything Pretty were the worst.

The one constant in my life, until now, had been that none of the people I lived with cared what I ate. Junk food was cheap and easy, so if I wanted to fill up on Doritos instead of salad, it was okay with them.

Until Rita.

Actually, if it weren't for her fetish about healthy food, I'd like Rita. At least she gives me some space and lets me make my own choices about clothes, books, and music. She's smart and makes me laugh—but she believes the axis of evil is sugar.

As I sidestepped around an especially deep pothole, thinking that maybe I would eat Twinkies for breakfast every day all summer, I almost missed the faded, water-stained bag that lay about three feet off the path. Its mossy green color matched the weeds growing beside the trail. I had already passed the bag when a tiny flash of light reflected from its zipper tab, and I realized I'd seen something that had not grown there.

I often picked up litter when I walked the trail after school. Usually I carried it to the trash or recycling containers outside Manny's Market.

It irritates me that people will use the trail along the creek, supposedly to enjoy Nature's beauty, and then, by littering, will pollute the very thing they have come to admire.

Over my weeks of trail walking, I've trained my eyes to search out man-made materials, those jarring bits of color that don't belong near the path. Expecting the usual candy wrapper or soda can, I stepped back to pick up the item that had caught my eye.

It wasn't litter.

The cloth bag blended into the landscape as if it had been lying there for a long time. I wondered how many times I'd walked past and not seen it.

I brushed off the dirt, pulled open the zipper, and looked inside. The bag held bundles of twenty-dollar bills!

"Whoa," I said. I looked around, half expecting someone wearing a ski mask to leap out from behind a tree, point a gun at me, and say, "Drop it right there."

No one leaped.

Sometimes I meet other people on the trail, often walking their dogs, but this morning I was alone. A slight breeze rustled the leaves; a bird called to its mate. I sat on the ground and counted the money: eight hundred and twenty dollars!

My hands shook as I stuffed the cash back inside the bag.

I zipped the bag, then stuck it inside my T-shirt, hoping the bulge wasn't obvious. I tucked the shirt into my jeans, to be sure the bag didn't slide out.

All thoughts of a Twinkie vanished as I ran back to Rita's house.

What should I do?

I knew two things for sure:

1. I had to try to find the bag's owner.

2. I wasn't going to tell Rita or my Hiss caseworker or anyone else what I'd found.

If the bag's owner showed up and could prove it was his money, I'd give it back. But if no one identified the bag, the cash was mine. It would be my secret, my ticket to find Starr.

Despite the warm June morning, goose bumps rose on my arms as I thought of my twin sister. No matter where she was living now, this was enough money to get me there, and give the two of us a fresh start, together.

All I had to do was find her.

2

Back in my room, I pulled the beat-up brown suitcase out from under my bed. It contained everything I wanted to remember about my life, which wasn't much. The most important item was a photograph of Grandma holding her little dog. I stood on one side of Grandma, and Starr stood on the other. We were three years old, wearing matching white shorts and pink T-shirts. Wispy ponytails on the sides of our heads were held in place by bright pink ribbons. Both of us grinned at the camera.

My dad had vanished before Starr and I were born, and if Mama knew where he was, she never told. Our last name, Skyland, was the same as Grandma's, and we all lived with her. A few days after the picture was taken, Grandma and Mama died in an auto accident. I don't know what happened to the dog. Maybe he had been in the car, too.

Starr and I didn't go to the funeral. Instead we played in the church's nursery room, supervised by a bored teenager whom we did not know. We were building towers with blocks and knocking them over when the service ended.

Starr and I were taken away in separate cars; I never saw my sister again.

Nobody mentioned Starr to me after that. She had been my constant companion, my playmate, the only person who could understand everything I said because we often spoke what Mama called "twin talk," a shortcut language that only the two of us knew. Then Starr disappeared, just like Mama and Grandma had disappeared a few days earlier.

I remember looking at the night sky through the car window as I was driven to my new home with my mother's great-aunt Cora. I wished Starr were sitting beside me, and I wondered where she was. I felt as if half of me was missing.

Even then, Twinkies were my favorite treat. I always nibbled the top off first, then scooped out the cream filling with my tongue. Grandma had often made me giggle by singing "Twinkle, Twinkle, Little Star" to me, changing the lyrics to "Twinkie, Twinkie, little star."

As I gazed at the sky that night and thought of my sister, I silently sang my own version:

"Twinkie, Twinkie, little Starr. How I wonder where you are." Of course I was too young to know that my twin's name was spelled with a double *r*. All I knew was that the song made sense to me.

Since then I had repeated the ditty every time I saw the first star in the evening sky. It was my mantra; it showed that I remembered my sister even though I didn't know where she was.

Great-aunt Cora was ten years older than her sister, my grandma, and had an ailing husband. A three-year-old proved to be more than she could cope with, so she talked her son, Jerod, into taking me. Jerod lived alone and had no desire to share his life with a little kid. Most nights I cried myself to sleep, missing Mama, missing Grandma, missing Starr.

Eventually, I ended up as a ward of the state. Jerod had taken me to Nebraska with him, and then left me behind, locked in an empty third-story apartment, when he moved again. By then I was four—only four but already too familiar with loneliness and loss.

When I woke up alone that morning, and saw that all Jerod's clothes were gone, my first thought had been, *Where will I live now?* I tried to open the door but the knob wouldn't turn. I thought I was locked in.

Mama had taught me to call 911 in an emergency. "Don't call unless someone's very sick, or there's a fire, or a burglar," she had said. I sat on the floor with my back to the locked door. I wasn't sick; there was no fire or burglar. I waited.

Did anyone know I was in the apartment? I waited for what seemed a long time, but no one came to get me. Even though I wasn't sick, I decided to call 911, but when I picked up the phone, there was no dial tone. The line had been disconnected.

I was hungry, and the only way to get food was to let someone know I was there. I found a blue towel crumpled on the bathroom floor. I opened the apartment window on the street side, and waved the towel out the window until a woman pushing a baby stroller looked up and noticed me. "I'm hungry!" I called.

"Are you alone?" she asked.

"Yes. I'm locked in."

"I'll get help," she said, and took a cell phone out of her pocket.

Ten minutes later, two police officers told me how to turn the small lever in the center of the doorknob to unlock the door. When it opened, one officer squatted down so he could talk directly to me. "What's your name, sweetheart?" he asked.

"Sunny Skyland."

"Where is your mother?"

"She died."

Those were the only questions I was able to answer. I didn't know Jcrod's last name, or where he had gone. I didn't know who my father was. I had no address and no phone number.

Nine years later, sitting in my room at Rita's house, I still felt hollow inside when I remembered how the police officers took me with them and told me not to worry, that I'd be going to a foster home soon. One of them bought me an ice-cream cone, but her kindness didn't make me feel less alone.

My old suitcase contained the clothes I'd been wearing that day. I'm not sure why I kept them. They hold no happy memories, but somehow they prove that I have a past, that I came from somewhere. Someone had bought that flowered yellow sundress for me; someone had buckled those white sandals onto my feet. Someone had cared, at least a little bit.

The suitcase also contained a magazine article that I had read and clipped several years earlier about twin boys who were separated as babies and reunited as adults. I had read it so many times, I could have recited it from memory.

A friend of one twin saw a man in a restaurant who looked so much like his friend that he approached the man's table and asked if he had a brother.

The man said, "No."

"I'm sorry to have bothered you. It's uncanny, how much you resemble my friend. I would have sworn you were his brother."

As he turned to leave, the other man asked, "Was your friend adopted?"

It turned out that he was.

This conversation led to a meeting of the look-alikes where the two men discovered they had been born on the same day and had been adopted from the same agency. Further research proved that they were identical twins.

I didn't know if Starr and I were identical or fraternal twins, but ever since I had read that article, I had daydreamed about someone coming up to me and asking if I had a sister. This stranger would swear that I looked exactly like someone she knew, and that someone, of course, would turn out to be Starr.

It made a good daydream, but I've learned that if you want dreams to come true, you have to take action. Sitting around and hoping someone might look at me and notice a resemblance to Starr was not likely to produce my twin. If I was ever going to find her, I needed to do it myself.

I put the bag of cash at the bottom of the suitcase, laid my belongings on top, and added a pile of school papers that I'd brought home the day before. I was pretty sure Rita wouldn't snoop in my things, but the suitcase didn't have a lock and if it got opened, I wanted the bag of money to be well hidden.

I shoved the suitcase back under my bed and went downstairs, humming "Twinkie, Twinkie, little Starr." Usually the tune made me sad and lonely. That day it made my heart soar.

I was going to find Starr. Somehow, some way, I would find my sister and when I did, I would finally have a family again.

3

That afternoon I went to the office of the local paper and paid cash for a classified ad. "Found money. To claim, identify amount, what it's in, and where you lost it."

I didn't want anyone to call Rita's house, so I used my e-mail address. Rita gave me an account on her computer, with my own e-mail address, even though I didn't have anyone to write to. I knew I'd be the only one who would read any responses to the ad.

I placed an identical ad on Craigslist, and then started watching my e-mail. I got one response right away that said, "I lost my rent money and I am going to be evicted tomorrow. I don't know where I lost it. You are my only hope. Please help me. Angie."

I noticed the writer did not say how much was lost, nor did she mention the zippered bag, so I figured this message was not from the rightful owner. Probably Angie hadn't lost any money at all but thought she could trick me into parting with what I had found. Well, Sunny Skyland is not easily tricked.

The newspaper ad ran the next afternoon. I checked the paper to be sure it was right.

My second response came a day later. It said, "The money is mine. I had it in my pocket and I'm not sure exactly how much there was, but now it's gone. I could have dropped it anywhere. I can meet you tonight to get it back, just tell me what time and where, and I'll be there."

I'll bet you will, I thought. How stupid do people think I am? If anyone had lost eight hundred and twenty dollars that was in a zippered bag, the bag is the first thing they'd tell me about.

I let both ads run for a week. A few more responses arrived, all equally unbelievable. As the days went by and there was no legitimate claim, my excitement grew. I started a list of things I wanted to tell Starr after I found her.

One e-mail said, "That money was left to me by my fathur who died of hart falure yesturday. It is all I have in the wurld. Pleez do not rob me of my futur by keeping it."

I shook my head. The ad had been running for five days before that person's father died—if he had died.

At the end of the week, I replied to all the people I'd heard from. I wrote, "Sorry. The money was claimed by someone who knew exactly how much it was, and what container it was in." I didn't say that the someone was me.

Meanwhile, I had searched for Starr online. It wasn't the first time I'd done that, and the result was the same as it had always been. I found towns named Skyland and people whose last name was Starr and even a group of amateur astronomers, but there was no record of a Starr Skyland in Google or Yahoo or anywhere else. She was not on Facebook or MySpace or any of the other social networks. It was as if my sister had fallen off the Earth. I tried spelling her name with only one r, but that didn't make any difference.

It occurred to me that whoever Starr was living with now might have had her use their last name instead of her own. For that matter, they might have given her a new first name, too. Maybe she wasn't bouncing around in foster homes like I was. Maybe she had been adopted.

I decided my best chance of finding her would be to return to where we had lived at the time of the accident. I would talk to people in our old neighborhood. Some of them might have been there when we were, and would remember us. They might know who had taken Starr, and where she is now.

I didn't know the name of the street where we had lived, but I knew the town because it was written, along with *Starr and Sunny, Loretta and Frisky*, on the back of that old snapshot. *Enumclaw, Washington*. I could also make out a house number, 1041, over the door.

According to the Census Bureau, Enumclaw has a population of eleven thousand two hundred people. That wasn't too big. Even without a specific street, I should be able to find someone who had known my mother or my grandma. I could go to every street in town and find number 1041. I could stop at the high school, and ask to see old yearbooks in case my mother had been a student there.

Starr might still live in Enumclaw. Wouldn't that be something? While I was driving away with Great-aunt Cora, Starr could have been moving in with our next-door neighbors. Perhaps she still lived there, in number 1039 or 1043. It was possible.

I studied a map of the United States. I was approximately thirteen hundred miles from Enumclaw, Washington. The closest airport to there was Seattle, but I had already decided not to fly. Instead, I planned to take the bus. It would take me longer to get there, but it would be harder for Rita and Hiss to find me if I bought a series of bus tickets from place to place than if I got on a plane.

I knew from watching the news that flying requires photo ID, which I didn't have because the photos for student ID cards at my current school had been taken while I was still living with She-Who and attending a different school. Also, a kid flying alone and paying cash for a plane ticket might attract attention. Better to travel a short distance by bus, maybe stay over a night or two, and then go a little way farther.

I decided to leave Rita a note. Although she'd probably still report that I was missing, if she knew I had not been abducted but had left on purpose, the cops wouldn't issue an Amber Alert, and the media wouldn't broadcast my picture. A foster kid who runs away, especially one who has run away twice before, would not be newsworthy.

I didn't want to waste the time of the police and others who would look for me if they thought I was lost or the victim of a crime. I wouldn't tell Rita where I was going, only that I was okay and would be in touch. Rita had been nice to me, so I added, "I'm not leaving because of anything you did."

If the whole state wasn't looking for me, I had a good chance of getting away. Just to be sure, I decided to change my appearance.

I made careful plans, thinking through each step. I would leave on Friday morning because Rita taught yoga classes on Fridays and was always gone from eight in the morning until two-thirty. It was the longest period of time that I could count on being alone.

I checked the local Greyhound bus schedule. A bus left at nine-thirty. If I started the minute Rita went out the door, I could cut and dye my hair and make it to the bus depot in time. I'd be off the bus before Rita got home and found my note.

Taking twenty dollars from the bag, I headed for the mall to purchase hair dye. I had no idea there would be so many choices. I read labels and instructions for thirty minutes before deciding on the one that sounded the fastest to use. I didn't care how I looked; I only wanted to look different.

Once I was safely out of town, I planned to let my hair grow to shoulder length again, and revert to its natural light sandy color. In the meantime, it was going to be Deep Burgundy Brown.

On Thursday night, I packed my backpack. I had decided to leave my suitcase and everything in it, except the money and the picture. A girl carrying an old suitcase would be identifiable; girls wearing backpacks are on every corner. I wanted to be as inconspicuous as possible.

Three sets of underwear. Toothbrush and toothpaste. Shampoo. An extra pair of jeans and two T-shirts. Socks. Pajamas.

I put in my favorite red Nebraska sweatshirt, and then took it back out. It was too easily identified because I wore it a lot. Instead, I packed a UCLA sweatshirt that I'd bought for a quarter at a garage sale but had never worn. I didn't think Rita had seen it.

The bulky sweatshirt took up a lot of space, but I was afraid I might be cold without it, even though I also planned to wear my Windbreaker. I hoped to find an inexpensive motel every night, but I needed to be prepared to sleep outdoors, if necessary. Even in summer the nights can get cool.

I looked longingly at my hair dryer and curling iron but left them on the bathroom counter, along with my nail polish and my creme rinse. I would worry about beauty after I found Starr. For now, I needed to travel light, taking only the essentials.

Food. I should have some food with me for times when I couldn't buy any, but the backpack was nearly full. I took two PowerBars and an apple from Rita's cupboard.

I sat on the bed and tried to think of what else I would need. I put in a small notebook and a pen, in case I needed to write down an address or phone number or directions, and the flashlight that Rita had given me. It doesn't require batteries; you just wind it up. Rita had one in every room, in case of a power outage.

I looked around my room. Of all the foster homes I'd had, this room was the best. Before I came, Rita had tried to make it a room that a teenager would like and not a babyish room all pink and with ruffles. The bedspread was two tones of purple, with three big puffy pillows on top. A matching purple Lava lamp perched on the bedside chest. A radio and CD player sat on a small white desk. If Starr could be here, too, I wouldn't mind staying in this room.

But Starr wasn't here and there was no guarantee that Rita would let me stay, even if I didn't run away. There are never any guarantees.

———

I awoke early on Friday and went downstairs to eat breakfast with Rita.

"Not sleeping in today?" Rita said. "Do you have plans?"

"It's too nice out to sleep," I said. "I thought I'd go for a walk." I didn't add, *To the bus station.*

"Would you like to learn to play tennis?" Rita asked. "One of the women in my yoga class gives tennis lessons and she offered to trade me. She'll come to my class for free, and you and I can take free tennis lessons from her. What do you think?"

"I don't know anything about tennis," I said. "I don't even know how to keep score."

"Neither do I, but it might be fun to learn."

"Okay," I said. I felt like a rat agreeing to tennis lessons when I knew I was not going to be here, but I didn't know what else to do. If I said no, Rita would ask a bunch of questions about why not. The truth is, tennis lessons sounded great, and if I had planned to stick around I would have wanted them.

"No cutesy little white skirts, though," Rita said.

"Shorts and T-shirts," I said, and then quickly changed the subject. "What's so nutritious about oatmeal?" I asked, knowing that if I could get Rita started on healthy eating, she'd forget about tennis lessons.

"All whole grains are good for you," Rita said. "Oatmeal provides all of the B vitamins, plus calcium, iron, and vitamin A. It's high in fiber and low in fat." While Rita extolled the benefits of oatmeal, I tuned out.

Ten minutes later, she waved good-bye and left for her yoga class. I fought an urge to hug her before she left. I couldn't do anything that might tip her off that today was different from any other day.

The minute the car pulled out of the garage, I dashed upstairs, put my note on her bed, and grabbed the scissors and hair dye.

I snipped about three inches off my hair, which put it just below my ears. It looked pretty good on the sides, but the back was uneven. I didn't have time to try to fix it. It took over half an hour to dye my hair. I put the empty box and the hair clippings in a plastic bag, to throw in a public trash can. If I left them here, Rita would know what I'd done and would change my description when she reported me missing.

My hair was still damp as I slipped on my backpack. I took one last look around my purple bedroom and left. Maybe Starr and I would come back sometime to visit Rita. I would tell her that of all the foster homes I'd had, this one was the best. Except for the food.

4

The bus station was not actually a station. It was a small counter in the back of a drugstore. I'd been there a few days earlier to get a schedule, so I knew exactly where to go to buy my ticket. On my way there, I stuffed the plastic bag in the trash container in front of the post office.

I told the woman behind the counter where I wanted to go.

"How old are you?" she asked.

I knew from the Greyhound Web site that kids under fifteen couldn't travel alone, so I said, "Fifteen."

"One way or round trip?"

"One way." I thought she might wonder why a kid

my age would be going somewhere alone and not coming back, so I added, "I'm meeting my dad there. We're going to go camping and then he'll drive me home."

The woman printed out my ticket.

There was a display of candy, potato chips, and other impulse-purchase items next to the counter. I picked up a package of Twinkies. "I'll take these, too," I said.

"The bus should be here in about ten minutes," the woman said. "Have fun camping."

"Thanks. My dad and I do this every summer." The ease with which false statements rolled out of my mouth astonished me. I didn't have much experience in telling lies, but I seemed to have a natural talent for it.

Those lies didn't hurt anyone, I told myself. I'm only making it harder for somebody to find me.

I sat on the bench in front of the store and ate my Twinkies while I waited for the bus. Each time a car went past, I looked down at my lap so that the driver and any passengers would see the top of my head rather than my face. It was unlikely that anyone I knew would happen along, but I wasn't taking any chances on being recognized.

The bus rolled in right on time and disgorged two young men wearing Chicago Cubs T-shirts. I climbed aboard, handed the driver my ticket, and started down the aisle.

I had hoped for a seat by myself, but that wasn't a choice. There were double seats on each side of the aisle and at least one seat in each section was occupied. I wanted to sit toward the front. Did I want to sit next to a white-haired woman who was reading a paperback book, a teenage boy listening to his iPod, or a tired-looking young woman holding an infant? I chose Granny.

I took off my backpack and held it in my lap. Since I was not carrying a separate purse, I had decided to hang on to the pack at all times, rather than put it in an overhead luggage space or in the storage area under the bus. I couldn't chance losing my eight hundred and twenty dollars, which, after the hair dye, bus ticket, and Twinkies, was down to seven hundred sixty-nine dollars and change.

As soon as I sat down, the woman beside me closed her book and smiled at me. I could tell she wanted a nice long chat. Even though I was quickly becoming a world-class liar, I did not relish making conversation with her for several hours, so I smiled, pointed at my throat, and said hoarsely, "Laryngitis. Can't talk."

"Oh, you poor dear," she said. She opened her purse, dug around, and came up with a cough drop. "Maybe this will help," she said.

I mouthed *thank you*, unwrapped the cough drop, and put it in my mouth. Then I leaned my head back against the seat, closed my eyes, and pretended to fall asleep. After a few minutes, I opened my eyes a slit, just enough to see that my seatmate was reading her book again.

Although I was too wired to actually sleep, it was pleasant to ride along with my eyes closed. I imagined how it would be when I found Starr. I pictured her initial surprise, and then her joy. I saw us throwing our arms around each other and exclaiming at how much we still looked alike, even with my new hair color.

She would tell me how much she had missed me, and how she had hoped to find me someday.

We would probably stay up all night the first night, telling our life stories. Maybe we'd discover that we like to do all of the same things.

In the article about the twins who had been separated at birth, then reunited as adults, it had turned out they liked the same food, played the same sports, and had similar jobs. They had even married people with the same first name! I wondered if Starr loved Twinkies.

When the bus stopped at the next town, my seatmate got out. After that I had the space to myself, so I didn't have to pretend to sleep anymore. I watched out the window, each mile taking me closer to Starr.

I arrived at my destination at two o'clock, wishing I could go farther. It seemed too early in the day to quit traveling. The bus stopped at a small diner, which served as the depot, and the driver announced that there would be a half hour lunch break.

I sat on a bench outside the diner, eating an ice-cream bar and looking at my map. It was thirty miles to the next stop and eight miles to the one after that. I had figured if I bought a ticket to one destination, stayed there overnight, and then bought a new ticket to continue, it would make it harder for anyone to track me. But did it matter if the second ticket was purchased tomorrow or right away? Probably not. Maybe I should buy another ticket now, get back on the same bus, and keep going.

As I was trying to decide what to do, an orange school bus pulled into the parking area and a group of girls my age swarmed out and went into the diner. A harried-looking chaperone trailed after them, followed by the driver. The side of the bus said SCHOOL DISTRICT 432.

I looked at the empty school bus. I looked at the diner. All of the bus riders were inside.

I boarded the school bus, walked to the last row of seats, and slid in next to the window. I checked the floor, to be sure nobody had left a sweater or anything that would make them want this particular seat. There was nothing, so I slumped into the seat and closed my eyes. I was good at pretending to be asleep.

About fifteen minutes later, the girls began returning, two or three at a time. An older woman called out, "Get on board, girls. We're leaving in five minutes."

I heard talking and shuffling as everyone boarded the bus. I didn't dare open my eyes. I hoped there were enough seats that mine wasn't needed, which turned out to be the case.

"Sit down, girls," the woman said. "Clear the aisles so we can leave."

The engine started. If anyone had noticed me, they apparently decided not to wake me up.

The bus made a *beep beep* sound as it backed up, then it headed out of the parking area.

It wasn't until we were rolling down the road that it occurred to me that this bus might be going in the wrong direction. I had no idea where these girls were from or where they were headed. What if I ended up right back where I had started from this morning?

5

It's a good thing I didn't really want to sleep, because someone started singing, "Ninety-nine bottles of beer on the wall," and each verse got louder. By the time they got down to one bottle of beer, the noise level was equal to that of a rock concert.

Next the girls began yelling school cheers. "We won! Sis boom bun! Sunrise School is number one!"

After much screaming, clapping, and whistling, they shouted, "No joke! No jest! Sunrise School is the best!"

I had never been on a team, had never even played a sport. As I listened to the girls cheering for themselves, I wondered what it would feel like to be a part of such a group. Clearly they had won some sort of tournament.

Did they have medals, or a trophy? Would they be written up in the local newspaper tomorrow?

I wondered if Starr was an athlete. I had always thought if I could learn a sport, I'd like to do gymnastics or volleyball.

After another hour or so of raucous singing and cheering, the girls quieted down, and by the time the bus pulled into the parking lot of Sunrise School, at least half of them were asleep.

"Wake up, girls!" called the chaperone. "Time to get off the bus. Be sure you take all your personal items with you, and don't leave the parking lot until your parents have arrived to take you home. I'll be checking each of you off my list before you leave."

Uh-oh. This could be trouble.

I sat up, watching as the chaperone exited the bus and stood at the bottom of the steps with a clipboard. The first girl to disembark was met by an adult woman. "Hi, Mom," the girl said. "Good-bye, Miss Lilton." The chaperone made a checkmark on the paper that was on her clipboard.

The next girl pointed to a car and said, "There's my dad." Miss Lilton checked the name off her list.

One by one the girls got off and were greeted by adults. I noticed that one girl was still in her seat, sleeping soundly. When she and I were the only ones left, I hurried to the front of the bus, stepped off, and pointed across the parking lot. I said, "There's my mom, Miss Lilton." Then, before she could ask my name and look at her list, I added, "You'd better check the seats in the rear of the bus. Somebody's still asleep back there."

Looking flustered, Miss Lilton boarded the bus and headed toward the slumbering girl, while I walked as quickly as I could across the parking lot and around the side of the school. I ducked into a doorway to wait. When the bus pulled away, I peeked around the corner and saw Miss Lilton get in a car and drive off.

Nobody would be able to track me here. There was not one person in the whole world who knew where I was. That knowledge excited me and made me nervous at the same time. What if I got sick? What if I fell and broke my arm, as I had when I lived with Jerod?

Stop it, I told myself. *You're where you want to be, doing what you want to do. Don't spoil it by worrying.* Besides, I knew Rita's phone numbers. If I ever broke a bone or got in other serious trouble, I knew I could call her and she'd come.

I walked away from the school and kept going until I came to a main street. Looking both ways, I saw a strip mall to my left. There were fast-food restaurants, a gas station, and, only half a block farther, the Dew Drop Inn.

I ate a chicken sandwich and drank a chocolate milk shake, then went into the lobby of the Dew Drop Inn. "Has Mrs. Webster checked in yet?" I asked. "I'm her daughter."

The clerk said nobody named Webster had arrived.

"I'll go ahead and register then," I said. "She should be here shortly."

"Do you have a credit card?" the clerk asked. "A double room is sixty-nine dollars. Or you can get a single room with a cot for forty-nine."

"The single's fine," I said. "I don't mind the cot." I gave him cash, which seemed to surprise him, and he handed me the key to room nine.

As soon as I got to my room I opened my backpack and checked the map, happy to see that the school bus I'd stowed away on had gone nearly two hundred miles in the direction I needed to go. I was a whole lot closer to Starr than I'd been a few hours earlier, and it hadn't cost me anything for a ticket.

I couldn't afford many nights at fifty bucks a pop, though. It wasn't even a good motel. Not that I was used to five-star accommodations, but the carpet was worn, the bathroom tile was chipped, and the ancient air conditioner protruding from the window sounded like a NASCAR race. Well, the room would be fine for my purposes. All I needed was a bathroom, a bed, and some privacy; it had all three of those.

Tomorrow night I'd try to find a YWCA where I could rent a less-expensive room.

The next morning I asked the motel clerk to direct me to the Greyhound bus terminal. He raised his eyebrows. "I thought your mom was meeting you here."

"She called. She got hung up in a business meeting and said for me to catch the bus and she'll pick me up at the other end."

I must have been convincing, because the clerk told me how to find the bus stop. On my way there, I passed a fast-food restaurant; I bought an order of french fries for my breakfast. I started to order a Pepsi, but then, hearing Rita's voice in my mind, I changed it to an orange juice.

I carried my meal to one of the outdoor tables. Movement in the bushes that lined the parking area caught my attention as I ate. Looking closer, I saw a dog lying with his head on his paws, watching me. As I ate a french fry, the dog's eyes followed the movement of my hand to my mouth. He licked his chops.

I tossed a fry toward him. It landed in the dirt about three feet in front of him. I expected him to lunge forward and grab it, but instead he rose slowly, and looked cautiously around before approaching the food. He sniffed the fry, then raised his head and looked at me, as if asking permission.

"Go ahead," I said. "That one's for you."

The dog ate the french fry. Then he sat down and stared at me. I knew he wanted more.

Something about the dog appealed to me. He wasn't a cute little puppy. In fact, his muzzle showed some gray and he moved as if his joints were stiff. He appeared to be an unlikely combination of basset hound and black Lab, with long drooping ears and big sad-looking brown eyes. The fur on his face was black, with a tan spot over each eye. His legs seemed too short for his body, but he had a certain presence, a dignity, that belied the fact he was hanging around a fast-food restaurant, hoping for a handout.

His ribs stuck out like the pickets in a fence and it had been a long time, if ever, since he'd had a bath.

"Good dog," I said, and he wagged his tail.

I went inside and ordered a plain hamburger, just the meat and the bun. I carried it outside and broke it into pieces to cool. With the pieces piled on a napkin, I approached the dog. His eyes stayed on the hamburger as I came closer.

"Here you are," I said, and I put the food on the ground in front of him. Again, he did not lunge and gobble it all down. He stood, looked at me, and wagged his tail.

"You're welcome," I said.

He ate slowly, as if savoring the treat.

When he had finished, I extended my hand, fingers curled in a fist, so he could sniff me. His tongue came out and slurped my hand. I petted him then and he sat down beside me, leaning on me so hard that if I had moved suddenly, he would have fallen over.

Now what? I thought. How could I walk away and board a bus and leave him here with no way to get his next meal? But I couldn't take him with me, either. I was pretty sure dogs would not be allowed on the bus.

Unless it was a service dog. I might be able to convince the ticket agent that this was a service dog, except that every service dog I'd ever seen wore a special coat with a service-dog logo. This dog didn't even have a collar.

I sat for a while, petting my new best friend. After a few minutes I went back inside.

"There's a dog in your parking lot," I told the girl who had sold me the hamburger. I pointed through the window.

"He's there every day," she said.

"Do you know who he belongs to?"

"I don't think he belongs to anyone. He hangs around and eats food that people leave behind."

"Where does he sleep?" I asked.

She shrugged. "I don't know. In the bushes, I guess."

"He's a nice dog," I said. "Friendly. Has anyone tried to find his owner?"

"You mean, like, put an ad in the paper or make flyers for a Found Dog?"

"Right."

"Nah. He's been out there for a long time."

"How long?"

"Well, I've worked here for, like, three months and he's been here that whole time."

I stared at her. For three months she had watched that dog beg for food and she had never tried to help him!

"Could I have a cup of water for him?" I asked.

"We charge twenty-five cents for water."

"That's okay."

She filled the cup, and I gave her a quarter.

The dog slurped eagerly, sticking his tongue down inside the cup. I poured the last of the water into my hand, and he licked it. *He needs a bowl*, I thought. *He needs a collar and a leash.*

He needs me.

I knew it would take me twice as long to find Starr if I had a goofy-looking old dog tagging along with me.

"I'm sorry, dog," I said. "If I lived nearby, I'd take you home in a heartbeat. But I don't live near here. I don't live anywhere."

The dog wagged his tail, acting as pleased as if I'd said, "Come on, pal. You're going with me."

I don't live anywhere. What an awful thought! It made me sound like one of those homeless people who shuffle along pushing a stolen shopping cart that contains everything they own.

I wasn't really homeless, not like those street people. I could always go back to Rita's and, even though she'd be mad at me for running away, I knew she'd take me back. Rita would probably take the dog, too.

I patted the dog, daydreaming about showing up at Rita's with this big old mutt.

"Who's your friend?" Rita would ask, and I would say he had followed me home, uninvited, and she'd know I was pretending and wouldn't care.

No! I pushed the image out of my mind. First I had to find Starr. Then the two of us would come back here and, if the dog was still hanging around, we'd adopt him and take him home—to my real home, with Starr.

I stood and walked away from the dog. I didn't look back until I reached the corner.

The dog was right behind me.

"You can't come," I said. "Stay!"

He hung his head.

His tail drooped.

My heart broke.

I knew exactly how he felt. I remembered all the times I had felt unwanted, times when I desperately wished to be welcomed and cherished. How could I do to him the very thing that had hurt me the most?

I couldn't. He was a stray, like me. We strays need to stick together.

6

We were standing in front of a supermarket. "I'll be right back," I said. "Sit." To my surprise, the dog sat down. "Stay," I said. The dog watched me go inside. I found the aisle that had pet supplies, and I bought a collar, a leash, a water bowl, and a box of dog biscuits. I also got a small box of plastic sandwich bags so that I could clean up after the dog. One of my pet peeves on the trail by Rita's house was people who left their dogs' poop behind for other people to step in.

I fastened the collar around his neck and snapped the leash on. I opened the box of biscuits and gave him one.

"You need a name," I said.

The dog crunched his biscuit.

"Maybe it should have something to do with the sky," I told him. "I'm Sunny and my sister is Starr and our last name is Skyland."

I thought of sky words: moon, cloud, blue. The dog's tan and black color suggested Earth words, not sky words. I saw that he had been neutered.

"Somebody loved you once," I said, "the same as me."

The dog's tail thumped the ground, making me smile.

"Now someone loves you again."

I crammed the box of biscuits into my backpack and put the pack on. I picked up the leash and walked down the sidewalk. The dog trotted at my side as if I had spent the last month teaching him to heel.

Maybe I could name him after one of the planets. Mars was the god of war; this dog seemed too peaceful to be called Mars. Venus was a goddess; I couldn't saddle a boy dog with a girl's name. Mercury didn't seem right, either. A dog named Mercury should be silver colored, and a fast runner. This dog plodded. Neptune? Uranus? Saturn? None seemed quite right.

Next I thought of Pluto. This old boy didn't look anything like the Disney cartoon dog Pluto, but I had always liked those old cartoons. What I didn't like was that Pluto is no longer considered a planet. Back in third grade when I had memorized the list of planets, Pluto was one of them. Pluto had been discovered in 1930 and had been a planet ever since until, all of a sudden, I heard that it wasn't a planet any longer.

How can the scientists arbitrarily get rid of a planet? How can an important part of the solar system be demoted? It seems to me that once a planet is called a planet there should be no mind-changing allowed. The same with dogs, and kids. Once you were part of somebody's family, you should get to stay forever.

I didn't want to name my dog after a planet that had lost its status. This dog was too good for that. Maybe I should name him after a constellation. Orion? Ursa?

The word *comet* popped into my head. I liked that because comets have tails. But comets orbit the sun, streaking across the heavens. This dog wasn't going to streak anywhere.

I decided to forget sky words and try to think of a name that fit the dog's looks and personality. His black fur was accented with the colors of caramel and dark chocolate. He had a sweet personality.

Snickers, I thought. I could name him after my favorite candy bar. It even starts with an *S*, the same as Sunny and Starr.

I said it aloud, trying out the sound. "Snickers."

He wagged his tail.

"Good dog, Snickers," I said. "After we find Starr, I'll get you one of those little tags to hang on your collar. I'll have it engraved SNICKERS, with my phone number on it, in case you ever wander off."

It did not appear likely that Snickers would wander off. Since he stayed as close to me as he could get, a more apt name might have been Velcro.

I'd never had a dog. She-Who had a cat, a big white Persian named Snowball, but he wasn't very friendly. He kept to himself, probably because he didn't like She-Who, even though she fed him. I didn't blame him. She fed me, too, and I didn't like her, either.

I didn't remember Grandma's dog, the one that was in the picture with us, but I'd always thought how great it would be to get a dog someday. I hadn't planned to do it when I was on the road alone, but you can't always anticipate what's going to happen.

In my experience, unplanned events were usually bad and often began with a foster parent saying, "Sunny, there's something I need to tell you," which meant I was going to be uprooted again. This time, finding Snickers, was good. He had been my dog for less than an hour and I already knew we'd be together for as long as he lived. No matter what else happened, we'd always have each other. I wondered if this is how it feels when you truly belong to a family.

———————

The bus ticket counter was in a health food store. I tied the leash around the leg of a park bench in front of the store, said, "Stay!" and went inside.

I walked past the bins of oat bran and wheat germ. Organically grown produce lined one wall. Instead of Twinkies, there were sugar-free carob cookies. Yuck. Rita would have loved this place.

I picked up a bus schedule and saw that the next bus going west would arrive in an hour. "Do you know if dogs are allowed on the bus?" I asked the woman who was unpacking boxes of egg substitute.

"Seeing Eye dogs are," she said. "I don't know about regular dogs."

I had already decided I couldn't take a chance on trying to pass Snickers off as a service dog. There was too much risk that it would lead to being questioned by the authorities.

"This is a plain old dog," I said. "A pet. He's really well behaved."

"You'll have to talk to the bus driver," she said.

I had noticed a small park down the side street, so while I waited for the bus I took Snickers there for a walk. He loved sniffing the grass and the trees.

When Snickers squatted to do his business, I saw a young woman with a toddler frown at us. I removed one of the small plastic bags from my pack, slid my hand inside, and picked up Snickers's waste. I quickly turned the bag inside out and dropped it in a trash bin. The woman smiled approvingly, and I was glad I'd had the foresight to buy bags.

When the hour was almost up, we walked back to wait for the bus. Ten minutes later, it wheezed to a stop. I waited while the driver, a bearded middle-aged man, helped two people retrieve their luggage. Then I approached him.

"Excuse me," I said. "I'm planning to take the bus and I'm wondering if it's okay to bring my dog. He's friendly and well behaved."

"No dogs allowed."

"I could pay extra for him."

I saw the man hesitate and realized that any extra would probably go straight into his pocket rather than the bus company's coffers.

"He'll probably sleep the whole trip," I said.

"How big is he?" the driver asked, which seemed like a stupid question, since Snickers was standing right beside me.

I pointed, and the man seemed to notice Snickers for the first time.

"No way," he said. "I thought you meant a little lapdog. Too many folks are scared of dogs. I could lose my job if I let you take him on board."

I made my lower lip tremble and tried to force a few tears from my eyes. "He's the only family I have," I said. "My dad left years ago and my mother died and I need to get to my sister's house. I can't leave my dog behind. I just can't!"

"Save your acting for the movies," the man said. "I'm not risking my job over a mutt." He walked away from me and entered the coffee shop on the corner. When he returned carrying a paper cup, he refused to look at me.

As I stood at the curb watching the bus pull away, I got a face full of exhaust fumes, but they weren't the only reason I felt sick. What was I going to do now?

I walked to the coffee shop and sat at one of the outdoor tables. I spread my map out, found where I was, and calculated how much farther I had to go. More than nine hundred miles. Could I walk that far? Could

Snickers? If we made twenty-five miles a day, it would still take over a month.

I had enough money for a month's worth of food, but where would we sleep? I had no sleeping bag or tent and didn't want to carry them anyway, so campgrounds were out. I was pretty sure that places that rent rooms, such as the YWCA, would not allow a dog and even if they did, my money would run out before we got to Enumclaw. What about weather? Sometimes in summer there are thunderstorms and even tornadoes.

I thought briefly about hitchhiking but quickly decided against it. Too risky. I wanted to find Starr, and I wanted to keep Snickers, but I did not want to climb into a vehicle with somebody who I knew nothing about.

Maybe I could board Snickers at a kennel and then come back for him. He would be safe and fed while I continued my journey on the bus. As soon as I found Starr and had made plans for my permanent home, I would retrieve Snickers and take him to live with me. I wondered how much it cost per day to board a dog.

I tied Snickers's leash to the table leg, went into the coffee shop, and asked if I could look at a phone directory. I turned to the Yellow Pages and looked under kennels.

When I saw an ad for dog boarding, I wrote the number in my notebook, untied Snickers, and found a public pay phone.

"How much do you charge to board a dog?" I asked, when Kanine Kennels answered.

"How much does your dog weigh?"

"I don't know."

"The charge varies, depending on if the dog is Small, Medium, Large, or Extra-large."

"I think he's mostly bassett hound with some black Lab."

"That would be considered a large dog. It's thirty-five dollars a day."

I gulped. "Where would you keep him?"

"We have six- by ten-foot covered kennels with concrete floors. Each dog gets a blanket to sleep on unless you bring his own bed."

"Would you take him out for walks?"

"Twice a day."

"Thanks," I said. "I have to think about it."

Mentally, I marked off a six- by ten-foot space. It wasn't very big, especially when I tried to imagine Snickers inside it.

It wasn't cheap, either. It would probably be at least two weeks before I could bail him out. That would be four hundred ninety dollars! It might take longer than two weeks to locate Starr, and then come back to get Snickers. Meanwhile his stiff old body would be resting on hard concrete. Even with a blanket, that didn't sound comfortable.

Snickers nudged my knee as I stepped out of the phone booth. I scratched him behind his ears while his tail whacked the ground. I looked into his brown eyes and knew he'd be miserable in a kennel. He'd think I had abandoned him, the same as everyone else. Even if I could afford to board him, there had to be a better solution.

I looked at my map again. If I took an older two-lane road, rather than the highway, it was twelve miles to the next small town. Snickers and I could walk twelve miles. It would give me time to think of a plan, and I'd end the day closer to Starr than when it began. Not as close as I had hoped, but twelve miles was better than nothing.

Before we left, I filled Snickers's bowl with water in the coffee shop's restroom and carried it out to him. After he drank, I used what was left to water a shrub.

It felt good to walk briskly along with Snickers at my side. Maybe Rita was right about exercise. She always said it was good for the mind, as well as the body, and I did feel optimistic as I headed down the road. I still didn't want to try to walk all the way to Enumclaw because it would take too long, but maybe I should walk whenever there were short distances between towns, just to stay in shape. It would be like training for a sport, except I would be accomplishing an even greater goal—finding Starr.

7

Unfortunately, Snickers was not up to a twelve-mile walk. After an hour of walking, Snickers began lagging behind instead of walking beside me. He didn't limp, exactly, but he walked more and more slowly, as if his legs hurt. I realized an old dog who had been sleeping outside with no medical care probably had arthritis. Maybe his joints ached, and if he had been accustomed to spending his days in the bushes next to the restaurant's parking lot, where he got little exercise, he was badly out of condition. The pads on his feet were probably sore by now, too.

I needed to find my twin sister, but Snickers needed a nap.

Flat fields stretched as far as I could see. Farm country. I didn't know what crop these fields were. Potatoes? Soybeans?

I sat on the shoulder of the road, at the edge of a plowed field. Snickers sank down beside me, heaved a sigh, and closed his eyes. The air smelled dusty, as if it had not rained for a long time. I dug my hands into the dry dirt between two rows and let it sift through my fingers.

The rural setting felt peaceful and spacious—and lonely. I wondered what Rita was doing, and hoped she wasn't too worried about me. I wished I had a way to let her know I was okay without also giving away my location.

If I saw a café with Wi-Fi in one of the towns ahead, maybe I'd ask someone with a laptop if I could send an e-mail. I didn't think that could be traced to the town it came from, only to the person who had the e-mail account. If the police asked the service provider where the person who had the account lived, did AOL, or whoever the account was with, have to reveal it? I wasn't sure. Better to be safe and not send an e-mail at all.

While Snickers slept, I examined the bottoms of his feet. His toenails needed to be trimmed, but he had thick, tough pads that looked as if he could walk many miles on them without a problem. His muscles must have been what ached. I didn't know what to do to help that, except to let him rest.

I let Snickers sleep for an hour, then roused him and headed on down the road, walking until he trailed behind me on the leash again, rather than trotting by my side. We continued the day's journey on a one-hour-on, one-hour-off schedule.

Just before sunset, we arrived at a town that consisted of a water tower, a one-pump gas station, a feed store, a combination drugstore/hardware store, and a grocery store. No motels. At first I didn't think there was a restaurant, either, but then I saw a faded, hand-painted sign that said JUNE'S HOME-COOKED MEALS. June's restaurant turned out to be one large room at the front of June's house.

A bell jingled when I went in. A short, plump woman entered, wiping her hands on a purple towel. Her blond hair formed a frizzy halo around her head.

"Howdy," she said. "I'm June."

"I'd like to get a meal," I said.

"Have a seat."

She gestured at three round wooden tables that

seated four people each. The centerpieces consisted of a bottle of ketchup, a paper napkin holder, and a salt and pepper set.

I chose a table and sat down. I was the only customer.

"You have your choice of a grilled cheese sandwich or a bowl of chili."

"Grilled cheese would be good."

"Anything to drink?"

Since there was no menu, I asked, "What is there?"

"Hold on a sec, let me check," she said, and disappeared into the back room. When she returned, she said, "I have milk, apple juice, and water."

"Apple juice, please. And could I also get water for my dog? I have his bowl."

As I took Snickers's bowl out of my backpack, June walked to the window and looked out.

"Good gracious," she said. "Don't leave your dog out there like some poor relation. Bring him in. He can rest under the table."

"That would be great," I said. "Thanks."

I brought Snickers inside.

June rubbed his ears and said, "Well, aren't you a handsome boy? Just look at you! What's your name?"

"His name is Snickers."

"Snickers?" she said, as if it were a foreign word that she'd never heard before.

"Right," I said. "Snickers, as in candy bar."

"Oh, *that* kind of Snickers. I was thinking of a mean type of laugh."

She petted Snickers again, then headed back to the kitchen. Soon she returned with a plate of table scraps. "I thought Snickers might enjoy some leftover stew," she said.

Snickers stood as she placed the plate before him. He wagged his tail.

"It's for you, Snickers," I said. "Go ahead."

"Would you look at that?" said June. "He's trained not to gobble down his meal until you tell him it's okay? I never saw the likes!"

"I didn't train him," I admitted. "He just always waits until I say he can eat."

"Now that is the most polite dog I've ever seen," June said. "He's welcome here anytime." She poured water from a pitcher into Snickers's bowl. "You new in town?"

"Passing through," I said. "Is there a place to rent a room?"

"Are you alone?"

"No. I'm with Snickers."

June laughed so hard that she had to wipe her eyes on the bottom of her shirt.

I didn't think it was that funny, but then there probably isn't a lot of comedy in this town.

"Myrtle Fishby used to take in boarders, years ago. She might rent you a room. Depends on whether her Social Security check covered the utilities this month. I'll call her."

I could hear June's side of the conversation. "Myrtle? Do you want a tenant tonight? It's a young girl and her dog. I don't know; a funny-looking dog, with big ears. He's very polite. Yes, I did say a girl; I meant the dog is polite. The girl is nice, too. Just a minute, I'll ask her." She held the receiver against her chest and asked, "Are you staying only one night?"

"Yes."

"One night, Myrtle."

June spoke to me again. "It would be ten dollars."

"I'll take it."

"Okay, Myrtle. I'll send her over after she eats."

It was the best grilled cheese sandwich I'd ever had—golden brown with a buttery taste, and the cheese all melted and gooey and oozing out the edges. It was real cheddar cheese, too, not the "cheese food" they use for nachos at fast-food restaurants.

The apple juice was served icy cold in its can and tasted great with the hot sandwich. I wished I could have all my meals at June's.

"That was delicious," I said as I swallowed the last bite. "How much do I owe you?"

"Two dollars."

Only two dollars? For a home-cooked sandwich, a can of juice, and stew for my dog? I couldn't believe my good fortune. I laid three dollar bills next to my plate, and asked how to find Myrtle's place.

June pointed. "One block down, on the corner. The yellow house with the pots of petunias on the porch." As I left, June said, "I'm cooking breakfast tomorrow. Pancakes and eggs. If you're interested, come on down any time between seven and nine. You too, Snickers."

"We'll be here," I said.

Myrtle had turned on the porch light, so I had no trouble finding her house, even though it was dark by then. She led me to a small room furnished with one twin bed, a wooden chest of drawers, and a table lamp. A braided rug on the floor would work for Snickers. I handed her the ten dollars.

"You don't have to pay until you leave," she said.

"That's okay. This way you know you have it."

The sheets on the bed smelled of sunshine. Rita always

hung the sheets outside to dry, so the smell of fresh air made me think of her. Until I had lived with Rita, my sheets and pillowcases had always come out of a clothes dryer, except at Jerod's apartment, where they never got laundered at all. At first I had thought Rita was foolish to lug the wet sheets into the backyard and hang them on the clothesline, even if it did conserve energy, but once I got used to that fresh, clean smell, I found I enjoyed it.

I slept soundly, awakening once when a train rumbled through town and blasted its whistle. As I fell back asleep, I heard Snickers snoring softly on the rug beside my bed. I felt safe here and wondered what it would be like to grow up in a small rural town, to live one's whole life in a place where a dog gets invited into the restaurant and served a free meal of table scraps. That would be against all the Health Department regulations in every place I'd ever lived. It was probably against the rules here, too, but the difference was that here nobody cared.

The next morning as I ate scrambled eggs and blueberry pancakes at June's, she brought her cup of coffee to my table and sat down across from me. "Where are you headed?" she asked.

"Enumclaw, Washington," I said.

"You have kin there?"

"My sister. I'm going to live with her."

"How are you fixing to get there?"

"The bus, if the driver will let me take Snickers along. The last driver wouldn't allow him on the bus, so we walked awhile."

"Tell you what," June said. "I need to visit my aunt today and I'd just as soon go now, before it gets too hot. You and Snickers could ride along, if you want. It's about fifteen miles west of here. The Trailways bus stops there."

"That would be great," I said. "Thank you."

I helped her wash the dishes. When she put a CLOSED sign in the window, I said, "Aren't you worried that you'll lose customers if you close in the middle of the day?"

"If I'm not here and they're hungry, they'll wait until I get back. Where else are they going to go for a meal?"

We piled into June's Jeep and off we went, with Snickers's nose aimed into the wind and his ears flapping out behind him.

The town where June's aunt lived turned out to be a sad-looking cluster of houses, some unkempt mobile homes, and a large grain silo. A one-pump gas station appeared to be the only commercial establishment in town. The peeling paint and dirty windows made me wonder if it was open for business or abandoned.

"I'm afraid it isn't much of a town," June said as she pulled up in front of the dilapidated gas station. "The bus will be along soon, though."

"Thanks for the ride," I said.

"You be careful, honey," she said. "Stop for a meal if you ever get back this way."

Snickers and I climbed out. I watched June's car cross the road and turn left, disappearing behind a windbreak of trees.

8

There wasn't a real bus stop—no shelter of any
kind, no bench to sit on, not even a sign. I opened the
door to the gas station and went inside, where I was sur-
rounded by loud music, the kind the radio stations call
"golden oldies." I didn't recognize the song—something
with a saxophone solo. An old man in coveralls sat on a
high stool behind the small counter with his eyes closed,
tapping his fingers to the song.

"Excuse me," I said.

The radio band continued with the sax replaced by a
string section. The man swayed to the beat, a half-smile
on his lips.

I spoke louder. "Excuse me!"

The man opened his eyes, frowning. He turned the knob on a large brown radio, and the music faded. "What can I do you for?" the man asked.

"I want to catch the bus, and I was told it stops here. Do I get a ticket from you?"

"From the driver. Just stand on the side of the road, and when the bus comes, wave your arms to signal the driver to stop. He'll pull over, and you can pay your fare then."

"How soon does it come?"

He consulted a large, round wall clock. "About fifteen minutes. Don't miss it; it only comes by once a day."

I thanked the man, and went back outside. Before the door closed behind me, I heard the music swell again.

The gas station provided a rectangle of shade that felt several degrees cooler than the air beside the road. I was tempted to wait there, but I feared I wouldn't see the bus in time if I didn't stand close to the road.

When Snickers started to follow me, I pointed to the shade and told him, "Stay!" There was no reason to make him swelter out in the hot sun while I watched for the bus. He lay down beside the building, and I wondered again about his past. Who had trained him? He kept his eyes on me as I walked to the edge of the road, but he didn't try to follow me.

As the mid-morning sun beat down, waves of heat echoed up from the asphalt. Sweat trickled down my neck, but I didn't bother to wipe it off. Thoughts of my room at Rita's house sneaked in the back door of my mind. Her house wasn't air-conditioned, but Rita closed all the windows and pulled the curtains shut early each morning to keep out the sun, so the house stayed cool. In the evening, she opened the curtains and the windows to let the breeze blow through. She called it Nature's air-conditioning, and it worked.

Voices approaching brought me out of my memory. I turned to see three boys emerging from behind the gas station. All wore jeans and T-shirts. The two in front, who looked about sixteen, swaggered and punched each other as they walked, full of their own importance. One was tall and lanky, with biceps that shouted "I lift weights!" His sidekick had an unlit cigarette dangling from his mouth.

The third boy was younger, maybe ten or eleven, and he lagged behind the other two.

The boys stopped when they saw me.

"Well, now, looky here," said the tallest one. He pointed at me. "Somebody new has come to town."

"Maybe we should introduce ourselves," said the second one. "I'm Hunker. This here is Zooman." He pointed to the tall boy.

"Hi," I said, then looked at the younger boy.

"I'm Randy," he said.

"We're the welcome committee," said Zooman.

Something about the older boys made me uneasy. Zooman's eyes were blank, and he seemed to look right through me. I wondered if he used drugs. Randy shuffled his feet and kept glancing nervously at Zooman and Hunker, as if he needed their permission to breathe.

I forced a small smile but did not say my name.

"What's in the backpack?" Zooman asked.

"Extra clothes. I'm going to visit my sister."

"Taking the bus?" asked Hunker.

"That's right."

"If she's taking the bus, she must have bus fare," said Zooman, "and maybe some cash for while she's at her sister's house." He stepped closer, with Hunker beside him. Randy stayed behind, making a circle in the dirt with the toe of his sneaker.

I clutched the backpack's straps and watched the boys warily.

"You owe me ten dollars," Zooman said.

"For what?"

"I'm the one who gives permission to catch the bus here. Ten dollars is the permission fee."

"No way," I said.

"You're refusing to pay the permission fee?" Zooman said, sounding as if he had never heard of such an outrage.

"Then we'll have to take it ourselves," Hunker said.

I stared at the boys but said nothing.

"Hand over the backpack," said Zooman.

I shook my head no.

"Didn't you hear him?" asked Hunker. "The man told you to give him your backpack."

My thoughts raced. Should I scream? Would the man in the gas station help me? Would he even hear me over his radio? Should I try to fight? Maybe if I kicked Zooman in the groin, he'd back off and the other two would follow. Or maybe that would only make them angry and they'd really hurt me.

I glanced up the road. No bus. No cars. No people.

Zooman held out his hand.

"Now," he said.

"This is a public road," I said. "Anyone can catch the bus here."

"Not without paying me first," he said.

Zooman and I stared at each other for a second. Then he lunged at me and grabbed hold of the backpack. He yanked so hard that one side slipped off my shoulder. I held on to the other strap and yelled, "Help!"

Hunker ran around behind me and tried to slide the other strap down my arm. I kicked at Zooman and missed.

A flash of brown and black fur shot out from beside the building, the loud barks startling all of us. Hunker dropped my arm. Zooman let go of the backpack.

Snickers rushed to me, then stood beside me, facing the boys, with his teeth bared. A menacing growl rumbled from his throat.

"He's trained to protect me," I said. "Take one step toward me, and he'll go for your throat."

The three boys backed away.

"Hey, we were only kidding," Zooman said. "We wouldn't really have taken your money."

"Yeah, right," I said.

"Nice doggy," said Hunker.

Snickers growled louder. He sounded vicious.

"Lucky for you he only attacks when I tell him to," I said. "Otherwise the three of you would be hamburger." I slid my arm through the strap and settled my backpack where it belonged.

The boys inched farther away, sliding their shoes on the dirt as if they wore skis.

I patted Snickers's head. "Good boy," I said. *We're even now*, I thought. I saved Snickers from a life of begging for scraps, and now he had saved me from being robbed and possibly beaten.

When they were about fifteen feet from me, the three boys turned at the same time, like a school of fish, and ran down the road. As I watched them, I saw the bus approaching in the distance. The boys dashed toward it, shouting and waving their arms.

Oh no, I thought. *Don't tell me they're going to take the same bus I am. If they get on, maybe I should try to find June and stay at Myrtle's house another night.*

The driver stopped beside the boys and opened the door, but they did not board the bus. I couldn't hear what the boys said, but the door quickly closed again and the bus drove forward. I saw the boys watching me and wondered what they had told the driver.

I waved my arms over my head. The bus slowed but didn't come to a complete stop.

As it rolled up beside me, the driver shouted through an open window, "The next time you kids flag me down when you aren't going anywhere, I'm calling the cops!" Then he stepped on the gas and pulled away.

"Wait!" I shouted. I ran a few feet after it, but the bus kept going.

While I watched the rear of the bus grow smaller in the distance, I heard the three boys laughing hysterically as they loped off in the opposite direction.

I stood there with the sun beating down on me and wondered why some people are so mean. Those boys knew that if they hailed the bus but didn't get on, the driver would be unlikely to stop for me. I could see why the driver assumed I was with them; what I didn't understand was why the boys wanted to make me miss my ride. Was it because Snickers had foiled their attempt to rob me? Did causing trouble for me make them feel superior? Or was it simply that they were bored and unhappy and not smart enough to figure out better ways to use their time?

I sighed. There was no way I would wait here twenty-four hours for another bus to arrive. I didn't want to spend twenty-four more *seconds* in the same town with those delinquents. I really didn't want to go back to Myrtle's, either, even if I could find June. They lived in the wrong direction. I wanted to continue my journey. I wanted to find Starr.

"Looks as if we're going to do some walking again today," I told Snickers. I went back in the gas station.

This time the man saw me enter, and he turned the radio down. "Miss the bus?" he asked.

"The driver didn't stop. He thought I was playing a trick and didn't really want to get on."

"Were the Jenley boys out there again?"

"Three boys waved at the bus before it got to me, but when it pulled over, they didn't get on."

"Yep. That would be Will Jenley's two boys and their cousin who's visiting from Alabama. They flag that bus down two, three times a week and then run off when the driver stops. I keep telling them, one of these days the driver's going to get fed up with their shenanigans and sic the law on them. Teach 'em a lesson." He shook his head. "Not the brightest bulbs in the box, those Jenley boys."

The one shelf in the glass counter held a few candy bars and other snack items for sale. There weren't any Twinkies, so I bought a Milky Way and a package of salted cashews. Then Snickers and I set off down the road together.

I glanced frequently over my shoulder, in case the three stooges decided to follow me, but I didn't see them again. Like most bullies, they disappeared as soon as there was a chance that they might get hurt themselves.

As I walked, I thought about what could have happened if Snickers hadn't come to my aid. I didn't think Zooman planned to hurt me, but he would have stolen all my money. He might have let me keep the backpack with my clothes in it, since he probably had no use for girl's clothes, but without any cash I'd have been in terrible trouble. I realized it wasn't smart to carry all of my money in one place.

As soon as I got away from town, and was certain nobody could see what I was doing, I stopped. I sat on the side of the road and opened my pack. First I poured some water in Snickers's bowl. The Milky Way was starting to melt, so I ate it. Then I folded some of the twenty-dollar bills into tight rectangles and put them in my shoes. When I slipped the shoes back on, I could feel the mounds of money under each foot's arch.

I wished I had a dog collar with a little container on it like rescue dogs wear in the mountains. If I had one of those, Snickers could carry some cash, too. I unsnapped the leash and put it in my backpack. Since Snickers stayed next to me, leashed or not, it didn't seem necessary to use it when no one else was near.

While Snickers finished slurping his water, I stuck some money in my jeans pockets. If anyone stole my backpack now, I'd still have enough funds to keep traveling. I'd still be able to find Starr.

With the cash distributed, we set off again. I never thought I'd be the kind of person who talks to her dog, but as we walked along, I found myself telling Snickers about my early memories of Starr.

"We used to lie on a blanket in the yard and watch for shooting stars," I said. "That's when Grandma first sang 'Twinkie, Twinkie, Little Star' to me, and I had a giggle fit and couldn't quit laughing."

As we plodded along the shoulder of the road, I tried to empty my mind of everything except memories. When people get hypnotized they sometimes remember events from long ago that they hadn't even known they could recall. I hoped that if I concentrated on scenes from my early years, new images might flood into my brain and give me some fresh clues about exactly where we had lived. It didn't happen, though. I only replayed the few events that I'd remembered all my life.

I soon ran out of my meager supply of family memories, so I told Snickers about Rita. "She got me a library card right away so I could read whatever I want," I said. "She let me use her computer, and trusted me not to look at sleazy stuff. When we shopped for clothes, she let me pick out my own and told me I looked pretty. If I had stayed there, I was going to have tennis lessons."

Snickers was a good listener.

"If I ever write my autobiography," I told him, "I'll skip all the years between when Mama died and when I went to live with Rita. I'll only tell the good parts of my life. First I'll write about Mama and Grandma and Starr; then I'll write about Rita. Next I'll tell how I found you, and finally I'll report the happy ending where I'm reunited with Starr. After that, I'll be so busy having fun and doing everything with my twin sister and you that I won't have time to write more chapters in an autobiography."

Snickers stopped walking. He looked around and whined.

"You can't be tired already," I said.

Snickers looked up at the sky and gave a short, high bark.

I followed his gaze and realized that the sky had grown darker while I was absorbed in my thoughts. A bank of clouds filled the sky ahead, darker clouds than I had ever seen. They had an odd greenish tinge, the color of an old sea turtle.

I realized the temperature had dropped, too. Even though I'd been walking at a steady pace, I no longer felt warm.

"Is it going to rain?" I said. "Is that what you're telling me?"

Snickers whined again.

9

A **wind rustled** across the road, and drops of rain spattered on my head and shoulders. Snickers poked my leg with his nose, as if urging me to hurry.

I know animals sometimes sense bad weather approaching before humans are aware of it. Maybe a severe storm was headed this way. I scanned the countryside around me for some place to take shelter. I saw rows of cornfields and, about fifty yards ahead, a big tree on the side of the road. Not too far beyond the tree, a ramshackle shed leaned sideways, as if trying its best to fall over. Probably it had once housed a tractor or plows or other farm equipment. Now it looked abandoned.

Even though its walls looked less than sturdy, the shed did have a roof, and right then Snickers and I needed a roof over our heads.

As I hurried toward the shed, the rain turned to hail. I ran, holding my arms over my head, as Snickers trotted beside me. A flash of lightning lit up the dark sky. Thunder followed the lightning. I wondered if Snickers had heard far-off thunder that my ears couldn't hear, and that's why he had barked.

Hail the size of gum balls pelted us, stinging my arms and the top of my head, as if the pieces had been shot from guns. Snickers yelped. By the time I reached the big tree, the ground was covered with round white ice balls, making it impossible to run. I tried to remember if you're supposed to stay under a tree during lightning, or get away from trees. I wasn't sure, but when I stood close to the tree trunk, most of the hail got deflected by the tree's branches before it could hit me or Snickers, so I stayed there. It seemed better to remain under the leafy canopy than to let huge hailstones pound us and risk turning an ankle or falling while we ran to the shed.

I knelt on the ground beside the tree trunk, with Snickers beside me. I took off the backpack. I put Snickers's muzzle on my legs, bent over him to protect his head, and held the backpack over my own head.

Some of the hailstones still hit us, but they were slowed by the leaves and did not strike with as much force as when we were out in the open.

The lightning and thunder continued. One huge lightning bolt zigzagged straight down, as if flung to earth by an angry god. Others bounced from cloud to cloud, seeking a place to penetrate. The wind increased. The earth vibrated. I could feel Snickers trembling.

"It's okay, boy," I said, trying to convince myself as well as my dog. "It's only a thunderstorm."

But was it? I had never experienced such a high wind before.

I had always counted seconds in a thunderstorm to estimate how close the lightning was: one, one thousand; two, one thousand. I'd been told that each second that elapsed indicated one mile; if I could count two seconds between the lightning and the thunder, it meant the lightning was two miles away. The thunder now followed the lightning with no space between them. Flash, *boom!* Flash, *boom!* The storm was no longer somewhere in the distance. It was here, beside us, all around us. I buried my face in Snickers's fur and pressed myself against him.

The wind whipped through the tree above my head, stripping leaves from the branches. My ears popped the way they do if I ride downhill really fast on my bike.

The hail stopped as abruptly as it had started, perhaps blown away by the strong wind.

Crack! A large branch snapped off the tree and fell onto the road.

Even with my backpack on my head and my palms pressed against my ears, the howling wind seemed to come from a boom box whose volume was on high.

Snap! Another branch broke off, this one dropping to the ground beside me.

Snickers began to pant, his sides heaving and his tongue hanging out of his mouth. His drool soaked my pant leg.

The noise increased to a roar. I raised my head to look toward the bank of greenish clouds that I had seen earlier, and gasped.

A tornado!

Beyond the shed, a funnel cloud whirled its way from sky to earth. I couldn't tell how far away it was. Not far. The tornado came toward me across the cornfield, its long, narrow funnel dangling down, twisting like a snake held by its tail.

I had seen enough nature programs on television to know I could not outrun a tornado. Besides, the wind was now so strong that I knew I would not even be able to stand up, much less run. I leaned hard against the tree trunk, slipping one hand through Snickers's collar to keep him close and grasping one strap of my backpack with the other.

Maybe the tree would act as a shield, protecting us from the storm's fury. If it didn't—if the tree was uprooted—I didn't think Snickers and I could survive.

The noise grew louder. It sounded as if a train track had been installed between two corn rows, and the train was rushing toward me at full speed.

The twister came closer.

Another branch snapped off, but this time instead of falling to the ground it flew across the road like a huge bird. I didn't watch to see where it finally landed because I heard a different noise, like fingernails scraping a chalkboard but magnified a thousand times. As I looked toward the noise, I saw the roof come off the old shed. A long, flat piece of rusty corrugated tin lifted up like a magic carpet and skimmed across the rows of corn, flattening them. It banged to the ground once, then rose again and continued its destructive journey.

Without the roof, the shed walls collapsed. If I had taken shelter there, the walls would have come down on Snickers and me. The center of the funnel swerved away from us after it hit the shed, but the edges swirled with such intensity that I felt as if Snickers and I were Dorothy and Toto in *The Wizard of Oz*.

One hand curled around Snickers's collar so tightly that my fingers cramped, but I was afraid to let go. With my other hand, I opened my backpack. I planned to snap the leash on Snickers and tie the other end around my waist. Whatever happened to us in this tornado, I wanted to stay together.

Like a giant scoop, the wind lifted up big chunks of the shed walls and sent them sailing into the air.

Then the wind ripped my backpack right out of my hand. The strap simply pulled from my grasp and the backpack rose as if it had sprouted wings.

"No!" I screamed. I grabbed at it, but it was far beyond my reach. All I could do was watch my backpack disappear into the distance, along with pieces of the shed, tree branches, and other debris.

Snickers panicked when I screamed. He jerked so hard that I could not hold on to his collar. He ran from me, racing blindly into the storm as if he believed he could run away from this nightmare.

He did not get far.

The whirling wind chased him, and as I watched in horror, a big branch dropped from the dark sky above Snickers and struck him in the head. He went down.

Feeling sick to my stomach, I tried to crawl to him, keeping myself flat on the ground while I pulled my body forward with my forearms. If he had been killed, I would never forgive myself. Even though I had no control over the weather and could not have prevented a tornado, I had brought him to this desolate place. I had made him endure a horrible storm, with nowhere to take shelter. As frightening as it was to me, I could only imagine how scary it must be to a dog, who did not understand what was happening. Snickers knew *sit* and *stay* and *good dog*, but he did not know what *tornado* meant.

The wind blew dirt in my eyes even at ground level, and bits of mud stung my cheeks. I kept my lips clamped shut, trying to keep the grit out of my mouth. I kept expecting some unknown object to drop on me, as it had on Snickers.

How could my trip to find Starr—the trip I had dreamed about for so many years—have ended like this, with my dog unconscious or worse, and me crawling in the mud while a tornado swirled around me?

Before I reached Snickers, the noise let up, and the wind became less intense. I raised my head and could not see the tornado. It had moved on or had worn itself out. Either way, it was gone.

The wind eased more. Several seconds elapsed between the lightning and the thunder that followed.

Snickers still lay motionless. I got up, ran to him, and
knelt beside him. I put my hands on his side, relieved to
feel the slight rise and fall as he breathed. "Good dog," I
said. "Good boy."

Now what? He needed to be seen by a veterinarian.
How would I get him there? He was too heavy for me
to carry. Not a single car had gone past since the bus, so
I couldn't wait to flag down a passing motorist.

Much as I hated to leave him, I decided the best
chance of helping him would be for me to walk back
the way I had come. I'd return to the town and ask the
man in the gas station to help me. Even better, I might
be able to find June. Maybe she had waited out the tornado in her aunt's basement or maybe the tornado had
bypassed the town.

If I couldn't find her, I'd ask the gas-station man to
help me find a phone number for June's Home-cooked
Meals, and I'd call her. June would come to get Snickers,
and help me lift him into her car. She would drive him
to a vet.

I worried that Snickers would come to while I was
gone. If he woke up and didn't see me, he might go

84

wandering through the countryside, looking for me. If he did that, I might never find him again.

I wished I still had my backpack so I could write a note and tuck it into Snickers's collar. That way if anyone happened to see him, they would know he wasn't a stray, that he belonged to me and that I would come for him.

But my backpack was nowhere in sight and I couldn't take time to search for it. I needed to get help for Snickers as quickly as I could.

I stroked his side. "I need to leave," I whispered. "I'm going to find help for you, but I'll return as soon as I can."

I kissed his forehead lightly. He didn't move. "Stay where you are until I come for you," I said. "Stay."

Blinking back tears, I walked away. When I looked at Snickers, he lay still, like a big brown and black rock in the field.

10

I picked up two boards that the storm had deposited in the field, and arranged them in an X at the side of the road so that I'd be sure to remember where Snickers was.

The scenery on my return trip was far different from what I had walked through only a couple of hours earlier. The cornstalks that had stretched tall in straight rows now lay broken, their tops angled in all directions. Some had been completely uprooted. Others looked as if someone had driven a large vehicle at random through the field, crushing everything in its path.

The green-black sky had brightened, but clusters of

melting hailstones offered further proof of the horrible storm that had passed through.

I walked faster without Snickers, jogging part of the time. I felt an urgency that I had never experienced before, a fierce desire to save my dog. Except for Starr, Snickers was the only family I had. I had quickly learned to love him, and now, when he was in danger, my fear that he might not make it made me love him even more. I had to find a vet for him as fast as I could.

This is farm country, I told myself. People probably have horses and cows, plus barn cats and family dogs. Surely there will be a veterinarian in the area. Snickers will get the treatment he needs. He will get well. He has to!

One bright spot: I still had part of my money. If I had left it all in the backpack it would be gone now, but by dividing it up when I did I still had half, enough to pay the vet. Maybe even enough to get me to Starr.

As I hurried forward, my eyes scanned the horizon, looking for the town. I was almost upon it before I realized that what I saw ahead was not what I had seen two hours ago. Instead of the gas station and the clumps of old houses, piles of debris littered the ground. The gas pump itself rested on its back, on the wrong side of the road, with the hose and nozzle missing.

A crumpled car lay upside down, squashed like an aluminum can that had been stomped on. Uneasily, I peered in the car's shattered window. The vehicle was not occupied. Either the driver and any passengers had managed to climb out and walk away or the car had been empty when it was lifted up somewhere else and deposited here.

The building where the old man had listened to his radio was only a heap of broken boards. Its tin roof was rolled back like the pop-top on a can of tuna, and pieces of pink insulation looked like mounds of cotton candy. Was the man buried under the rubble? Might he still be alive?

With my heart pounding, I approached what was left of the building. "Hello?" I called. "Are you there? Can you hear me?"

Nobody answered. I looked around. Where was everyone? Some of the houses on the other side of the road must have been occupied when the tornado hit. Were there survivors? Staying clear of a downed power line, I walked toward the houses, past a flowered sofa, an old refrigerator, and a baby's high chair that had three legs snapped off.

As I approached the closest house, I heard a hissing sound. I quickly looked around for a snake. Were there rattlers or other poisonous snakes in this part of the state?

I didn't see a snake, but the hissing continued. Then I smelled an odd odor and realized I heard propane leaking from a broken line. I'd noticed a white propane tank near every house, and wondered why they weren't painted green so they'd blend in with the landscape. Fearing an explosion, I skirted that house and approached what looked like a huge pile of kindling that had pieces of furniture mixed in with the wood.

A piece of paper fluttered down and landed in the dirt beside me. I picked it up. It was a child's drawing: a family of smiling stick figures with a bright sun overhead. SUZY was printed in wobbly block letters on the bottom of the drawing.

Where was Suzy now? What had happened to the people who lived in these houses? Where was June, and her aunt? I folded the drawing and put it in my pocket. The still air made it feel like a ghost town, and I shivered in spite of the heat.

"Hello?" I called. "Is anyone here?" As I zigzagged through the splintered wood and rain-soaked contents of the former houses, I heard a sound.

I stopped, listening. It came again, a faint cry. "Help."

I went toward the voice. "I hear you," I called. "I'm coming! Keep talking so I can find you."

"Here," said the voice. "I'm under here."

The voice came from beneath a heap of rubble, all that remained of one of the houses. I began to dig, throwing pieces of wallboard and roof shingles off to the side, trying to reach the voice.

"Don't worry," I said. "I'll get you out."

"Hurry," replied the voice. It sounded like a child.

When I tried to pry a piece of siding loose, I got a splinter under one of my fingernails. I tried to pull the splinter out with my teeth, but it broke off. Ignoring the soreness, I kept working toward the voice.

After I pulled away a large chunk of ceiling tile, I was startled to see the soft brown eyes of a cow looking at me. I had uncovered a large oil painting that, except for being dirty, did not appear to be damaged. I lifted the painting, shook the dirt off, and set it aside. If the owners of this home returned, they would be surprised to find their cow painting in such good condition when the rest of the house was demolished.

Beneath where the painting had been, I glimpsed hair. Human hair. I was looking at the back of someone's head. No wonder the voice seemed so muffled. The person was lying facedown in the dirt. I removed more debris until the whole head was uncovered.

"I see you!" I said. "Can you turn your head? You'll be able to breath better if you can turn."

The head turned slowly and I saw the profile of Randy, the youngest of the three boys who had tried to rob me. He looked at me for a second, then closed his eyes.

"I'll keep digging," I said, "until you can crawl out of there."

He moaned.

I tugged at the rubble that covered Randy's shoulders and back. When his arms were free, I said, "Can you raise up on your elbows and pull yourself loose?"

He struggled briefly, then started to cry. "My legs hurt," he said. "My legs hurt really bad."

"I'll dig them free," I said.

But I didn't.

I couldn't. When I yanked a piece of ceiling off Randy's legs, it revealed a cast-iron sink lying on top of him. The sink covered his legs from mid-thigh to mid-calf. His ankles protruded out the bottom at an unnatural angle. His legs were surely broken.

If I lifted the sink off him, I could fashion splints from pieces of board and make him more comfortable while he waited for medical help.

I tugged with all my strength, but I was not able to remove the heavy sink.

"There's a sink on top of your legs," I said, "and it's

too heavy for me to move it. I'm going for help. I'll send someone back to get you out of here."

"Don't leave me," Randy whimpered. "I don't want to stay here alone."

"Where are Zooman and Hunker?" I asked.

"I don't know. We came home to their house to get some lunch and we heard hail on the roof. I was in the bathroom when I heard Zooman yell, 'It's a twister! Run to the shelter!'"

Good, I thought. *Maybe there are other survivors who are still in a storm shelter.*

"By the time I got out of the bathroom, Zooman and Hunker were gone. When I called to them, they didn't answer." Randy spoke haltingly, as if it hurt to talk. "I stepped outside, but I didn't see them, and then the wind blew so hard I fell down, and then something landed on top of me and I blacked out." Sobs temporarily replaced words as he struggled for control. "When I woke up, I couldn't move or see and my legs hurt. I lay here, and then I heard you calling, and I answered."

I patted Randy's shoulder. How could the older boys have run to the shelter and left him behind?

"I'll get help for you," I said. "You need to lie as still as you can while I'm gone. I promise I'll find someone and send them here to get you out."

"Cross your heart?" he asked.

"Cross my heart."

Tears trickled down his muddy cheeks. "We were mean to you," he said.

I wondered if he was afraid I wouldn't really help him because of what had happened earlier. "Zooman and Hunker were mean," I said. "I don't think you wanted to take my money, but you were scared of them."

"I'm scared now, too."

"I'll hurry," I said. "I'll send help as fast as I can."

I left Randy pinned under the sink. I wasn't going to find a veterinarian here, or a doctor for Randy, or aid of any kind. I returned to the road and hurried back toward Snickers. I had spent a long time trying to free Randy, and my dog still needed help.

My arms ached from lifting and digging to get to Randy, and my fingernail throbbed where the splinter was lodged under it. I wished I could take a warm shower and then crawl into my comfy bed at Rita's house and have a nap.

As I headed back to Snickers, I thought back to televised news accounts of natural disasters. The Red Cross usually sent workers. So did the government, although I remembered that the government aid was often slow to arrive. After Hurricane Katrina, animal-rescue groups had gone to New Orleans to aid with injured or lost pets. Maybe that would happen here and an animal-rescue group would help Snickers. Not today, though. It takes a day or two for rescue groups to arrive. I wasn't sure Snickers could wait that long.

I should have spent some of my money on a cell phone. When I planned this journey, I didn't think I would want to call anyone. Who would I call? Now I wished I had considered the possibility of an emergency. I could have used a phone to call for help.

I'm coming, Snickers, I thought. *Stay where you are. I'm coming!*

I ran, even though my knees felt as if they would buckle at any moment. My breath came in short gasps, and a persistent pain jabbed my side, but I kept running. I ran toward Snickers, and away from the devastation I had seen. I wanted to run until I was miles away from this place. I wanted to run and run, until Snickers and I were safe.

Eventually I saw the boards that I had used to make my X beside the road. When I reached them, I turned to the right, to where I had left Snickers.

I saw only the empty field.

Snickers was gone.

11

My eyes scanned the field, searching for a black and tan dog. Instead I saw battered rows of corn and debris from the tornado.

Snickers must have awakened and gone to look for me.

Fear rose in my throat. Sometimes when an animal is sick or injured, it will crawl away and hide somewhere, and wait to die. What if Snickers had done that?

"Snickers!" I shouted. "Here, Snickers! Come, boy!"

Wouldn't he have smelled me and followed my scent? But if he had gone after me toward town, we would have found each other. Did the rain-soaked ground dilute my odor, making it harder for him to track me?

Perhaps he had gone back to the tree where we had waited out the tornado. That's where I had been when he panicked and ran. That's where he had last seen me.

I ran toward the tree.

Paw prints circled the base of the tree, and my hopes soared, even though I knew they could have been made before the tornado hit.

"Snickers!" I yelled again. "Here I am! Snickers!"

I heard him before I saw him—a soft whimper coming from a patch of corn that was still standing.

"Snickers!" I called, and then he emerged, walking slowly toward me as if it hurt him to move.

I ran to him, and threw my arms around him. Relief flooded through me as he licked my cheek.

I had told Randy I'd find help for him, but it was clear that Snickers was in no condition to travel and I couldn't leave him alone again.

Knowing I was as likely to find help by waiting here for it to arrive as I was by walking any farther with an injured dog, I decided to stay with Snickers until we were rescued, and then I'd direct the rescuers to Randy. Maybe he'd be found first. Search teams would look in the remains of a town before they'd hunt in a cornfield. I should have told him where I would be so that he could send help my direction if he got found before I did.

I sat on the ground, and Snickers lay beside me. The wound on his head had formed a scab, and there was a lump the size of an egg. I didn't touch it. I wished I still had my backpack so that I could give Snickers a drink of water and a dog biscuit. All I could offer him were words of comfort.

"Someone will find us," I told him. "There are probably people searching already, looking for survivors of the tornado. They'll find us before long. They'll help us."

I knew that I spoke the truth, and my heart filled with gratitude for these strangers who would come to our aid. There may be mean people like Zooman and Hunker in the world, but there are also good people who leave their comfortable homes and rush to help in times of trouble.

I stroked Snickers's fur. He put his head on my leg, closed his eyes, and sighed.

We sat like that for about an hour before I heard the helicopter. I stood and looked up, shielding my eyes from the sun. The helicopter approached from the west, flying low. It appeared to be following the road that Snickers and I had walked on. I could see two people inside it.

I waved my arms over my head, trying to signal the pilot and his passenger. The helicopter passed to my left, then circled back over me. I waved again, and watched as it hovered over the road and then slowly landed. Snickers began to pant again, afraid of the noise, and I held tight to his collar. The chopper blades sent swirls of dust into the air. A man jumped down and ran toward me.

"Are you okay?" he called.

"I'm not hurt," I yelled, "but my dog needs a veterinarian. He got hit on the head with a branch during the tornado."

The man stopped beside me. "An emergency shelter is being set up in an old school about ten miles west of here. I can give you a lift there," he said.

"What about Snickers?"

"The dog?"

I nodded.

"You'll have to leave him here. You can probably come back for him in a day or two."

"I can't leave him," I said. "He would try to follow me. He'd get lost."

"I can't take him in the chopper," he said. "I need to keep the space open for any injured people I find. We're not equipped to rescue animals."

"Then I'll stay here," I said.

"Don't be foolish," the man said. "I know you love your dog, but you need to get to the shelter where there's food and people to help you. What if another twister comes through?"

I had not considered that possibility, but I realized it could happen. Tornadoes sometimes come in bunches. Even so, I shook my head. "Snickers is my best friend," I said. "I can't leave him behind."

The man shrugged his shoulders, as if he thought I was making a huge mistake. "Suit yourself."

"Could you tell the people at the shelter where we are?" I asked. "Maybe someone could drive here to get us. Maybe even a veterinarian would come."

"I'll tell them you're here," he said, "but don't get your hopes up. In an emergency like this, most people are busy trying to find family and friends or helping those who were injured or left homeless. Destruction from this storm is widespread. A few miles west of here we saw three boxcars that had been lifted off the railroad tracks. You're lucky to be alive."

"There's a boy, Randy, who needs help right away," I said. "He's about two miles that way." I pointed. "A house came down on top of him. I tried to dig him out, but his legs are pinned by a sink that was too heavy for me. The town is destroyed; he's the only person I found. I think his legs are broken."

The man started back toward the helicopter.

"Wait!" I yelled, and he looked back. "I think there's a broken propane line near Randy."

"Thanks. We'll check that out." Just before he got to the place where he had to duck down and run through the wind caused by the chopper blades, he called back, "Are you sure you want to stay here?"

I waved, to signal he should go without me.

I stood beside Snickers and felt tears drip down my cheeks.

As the helicopter rose, I saw something fall from it and land in the dirt. I walked toward it, and found a bottle of water. My would-be rescuer had thrown down the one thing Snickers and I needed the most.

"Thank you!" I shouted as I held the bottle over my head. I knew he couldn't hear me, but I yelled it anyway. "Thanks for the water!"

The helicopter flew off, headed toward Randy.

I opened the bottle of water and took a drink. Then I cupped one hand and poured some water into it for Snickers. He lapped it quickly, wagging his tail. I thought about pouring some water on his wound, to clean it and try to keep it from getting infected, but I decided I should save the water for drinking. I didn't know how long it would be before we got rescued.

For a while I scanned the sky, watching for the helicopter to go back the way it had come. I was sure that two adults would be able to lift the sink off Randy's legs.

An hour passed, and then two hours. By now, I thought, they should have carried him to the helicopter and flown him to a hospital, or at least to a waiting ambulance. Maybe the closest hospital was not this way. Maybe they had flown Randy in the opposite direction.

While I watched for the helicopter, I also kept alert for the possible sound of a vehicle coming my way. I fantasized that a minivan drove up and a woman who looked like Rita jumped out and said, "I'm a veterinarian. I've come to take you and your dog to my clinic." It didn't happen, though.

The sun turned a fiery golden red as it sank below the horizon, casting an orange glow on the scattering of clouds. The temperature dropped, and I was glad for the warmth of Snickers beside me.

My stomach grumbled. I wished I had eaten the cashews instead of saving them in my backpack. I tried not to think about food, but the more I tried not to think of food, the more images of food danced in my mind. Mac and cheese. A chocolate milk shake. Pizza. Even one of Rita's healthy vegetable soup and salad dinners sounded good. I wondered if Snickers was visualizing a box of dog biscuits or a bowl of kibble or more of June's stew. I took another drink of water and gave some more to Snickers, hoping to fill our empty stomachs with liquid.

Darkness descended. I lay on my side, with my knees bent. Snickers curled next to me. He fell asleep immediately and began snoring softly.

I wondered if I should wake him up now and then during the night, because of his head injury. Once when a girl I knew had fallen off her scooter and hit her head on the pavement, her parents had been instructed to wake her up every two hours all night long, to be sure she was sleeping and not unconscious.

While Snickers slept, I lay there with my mind racing. I was sure I'd get to the shelter the next day. If nobody came to rescue us, Snickers and I could walk there. But what should I do when I got to the shelter? People would ask where I lived. They would want to know who my parents or guardians are. I couldn't give my real name.

I decided to say my name was Kaitlyn Smith. If asked, I'd say I had missed the bus and was walking when the tornado hit. That part was true. Although I was becoming an accomplished liar, I knew if I told too many untruths it would be hard to remember what I'd said and I would be more likely to be found out.

When I shifted position, Snickers opened his eyes and looked at me as if he wanted to be sure I was still there. Then he went back to sleep. Good. I wouldn't need to wake him on purpose.

I stroked his back and found that petting him relaxed me. Soon my eyes closed, too.

Several times during the night, I woke up because I was stiff. Even cuddled next to Snickers, I couldn't get comfortable and I longed for my bed at Rita's house, with the purple bedspread and the soft patchwork quilt. Thinking back, I realized how many things I had liked about living with Rita—physical things like the quilt and the computer access, but also intangibles, such as Rita's willingness to let me choose my own clothes and her sense of humor as she encouraged me to do homework. Rita had a curiosity about the world that made ordinary events more interesting. She carried binoculars in her car, in case she spotted an unusual bird. She always asked store clerks and waiters about their jobs. "You can learn a lot by listening to the people you meet every day," Rita said.

Two days before I left, I had found her knitting like crazy, and I asked her what she was making. "A bagel," she said.

I stared at her. "What?" I asked, thinking I had misunderstood.

"This morning I was toasting a bagel," she said, "and I thought it was the perfect shape to be a bracelet, so I decided to knit a bagel bracelet."

I thought she was crazy until I saw the finished

product. The next day, she held up her arm and said, "I finished my bagel bracelet. How do you like it?"

It was a round knitted tube, about an inch in diameter, made of a soft light tan yarn. Rita had sewn a variety of funky old buttons around the outside rim. It was unlike any bracelet I'd ever seen, and I loved it.

"Cool," I said. "Can you make one for me?"

"Sure. Go through the old buttons in my button jar and pick out which ones you want for decoration."

I wished now that I hadn't left before Rita had knit my bagel bracelet. It would have been perfect to remember her by. I wondered if she had knit a bracelet for me anyway, in case I came back. If Starr and I go to visit Rita, I'll ask her to knit matching bagel bracelets for us.

Thinking about Rita made me sad, and it occurred to me that I was a little bit homesick. How could I be homesick for a place that wasn't really my home? I told myself I only felt that way because I was hungry and tired and uncomfortable.

Tomorrow I would push Rita out of my thoughts and get on with my quest to find Starr. I felt sure that she had longed for me all these years, just as I had yearned for her. Once we were reunited, I would truly be home.

12

The sound of a vehicle approaching woke me. The sun had not yet risen, but the sky was growing light. I saw a pair of headlights coming toward me.

Snickers stood and shook, making his ears flap. I stood, too, and walked toward the road, waving at the lights.

A large black pickup truck, the kind with a backseat, pulled up next to me. The driver, a man in a baseball cap, leaned out the window. "Need a lift?" he asked. "There's temporary housing and food available about ten miles up the road."

"Is it okay to bring my dog?"

The man laughed. "They may not let him inside the building, but I don't mind giving him a ride. Hop in."

I hesitated briefly, wondering if I should ask him for identification. Under normal circumstances, I wouldn't dream of getting in a truck with a man I didn't know. Then I saw that he wore a white smock over his shirt; the smock said AMERICAN RED CROSS VOLUNTEER in big red letters.

He opened the passenger door. Snickers scrambled in first and sat between me and the man as if he had ridden there a hundred times.

"My name's Jake," the man said.

"I'm Kaitlyn," I replied, silently congratulating myself for having chosen the pseudonym ahead of time so that I could answer without hesitation. "My dog's name is Snickers."

"Where do you live?" he asked. "Should I drive you home instead of to the shelter?"

"I'm not from around here. I'm on my way to my sister's house, but I missed the bus yesterday. Snickers and I were walking a while and got caught in the tornado."

"You were outside?" he asked. "With no protection?"

"We sat under a tree to try to get out of the hail, and it ended up shielding us from the wind."

He looked at me as if I were the eighth wonder of the world. "You are one lucky girl," he said, "and your dog, too. Half the trees in the county were uprooted. The wind hit one hundred and fifteen miles an hour in some places. The next town east of here is gone, every building wiped out."

"I know," I said. "I saw it. I tried to dig out a boy who was buried in the rubble, but I couldn't get everything off him. I told a man in a helicopter where the boy was."

"That was you?" Jake said. "You're the one who saved the boy from Alabama?"

"You know about Randy?"

"They airlifted him to the hospital and he couldn't stop talking about a girl who he had been mean to, but she tried to help him anyway. The TV station is having a field day with the story. According to the reporters, you saved the kid's life."

I hoped that was true.

"They're trying to locate you, for an interview."

I immediately regretted saying anything about Randy. I certainly did not want a reporter interviewing me and broadcasting my picture.

"Please don't tell anyone else it was me," I said. "I don't want a big fuss."

Jake smiled his approval. "Well, that's refreshing," he said. "Most people mug shamelessly at a camera, trying to get on TV."

"I'm shy," I said. Then, hoping to change the subject, I asked, "Were there other survivors there besides Randy? I didn't see any people, but I didn't see any bodies, either."

"Some folks weren't home, and everyone else made it to the town's underground storm cellar. The siren that was supposed to sound the warning malfunctioned, but people saw the hail and wind and realized what was happening in time to get to the shelter. When you live in tornado country, you learn to watch the skies and be cautious. We're always supposed to stay in the shelter until the all clear siren sounds, but this time it never went off. They waited almost three hours before they finally tried to open the door, and then it was blocked shut by rubble."

"So nobody was killed?" I asked, thinking about June and the old man at the gas station.

"Nope. The only serious injury was the boy with the broken legs and the crushed pelvis, and he'll survive."

A crushed pelvis, too. Poor Randy. At least he was alive and had not had to wait alone too long after I left him. I wondered if he had told Zooman and Hunker's parents how the older boys had deserted him.

"Tornadoes are unpredictable," Jake said. "They hop about at random, creating chaos in some places and completely missing other spots. The town of Alliance, where I live, didn't even get the rain or hail."

"Is there a veterinarian near here?" I asked. "Snickers got hit on the head and was knocked out."

"He seems okay now."

"I'd like to have him examined, just to be sure."

"Maybe somebody at the school will give you a ride to a vet. I'd take you myself, but we were assigned territories to look for survivors and I need to stay in my area."

Jake's truck pulled up to an old brick school building. A banner draped over the door of what appeared to be the gymnasium said AMERICAN RED CROSS TEMPORARY SHELTER.

A big silver van, the kind where a window opens on the side for serving food, was parked in the yard. A car next to it had its trunk open and two women were unloading boxes of food and supplies.

"Are you hungry?" Jake asked.

"I'm starving. All I've had since breakfast yesterday morning is a candy bar and some water."

"Wait here," Jake said, and he jumped down from the truck and walked to the women who were unloading the boxes. A moment later he climbed back in the truck and handed me a sandwich wrapped in plastic wrap. "I hope you like ham and cheese," he said.

"Right now I'd be willing to eat cauliflower," I told him.

I unwrapped the sandwich, picked out the ham, and gave it to Snickers, who gulped it down without even chewing. I bit into the sandwich. "Yum," I said. "Thank you." I gave Snickers a couple of bites of bread and cheese, and ate the rest myself. No meal had ever tasted better.

As soon as I finished eating, Jake said, "I need to leave you here. I'm supposed to be out driving around, looking for survivors who need assistance."

"Thanks for your help," I told him. I got out of the truck, and Snickers jumped out, too. He followed me to the door of the school, and up the three concrete steps.

"Stay," I told him, before I opened the door.

Snickers obediently sat down on the top step and watched me go inside.

Rows of cots formed lines in the center of the building. People slept on some of the cots. A few people sat on others, talking quietly. Chairs lined the periphery of the room. A woman sat on one of the chairs, playing peekaboo with a toddler. Two little boys chased each other between the rows of cots until their mothers made them stop.

A table stood just inside the door, with two women behind it. The table held a notebook computer, lined tablets, pens, and a first-aid kit.

One of the women smiled and said, "Hello. Do you need a temporary place to stay?"

"Yes."

"Let's get you registered on our Safe and Well Web site. Sign in here, please." She pointed to a list of names, addresses, and phone numbers.

Stalling for time while I tried to figure out a reason to refuse, I said, "The what?"

"The Red Cross maintains a Safe and Well Web site. After a disaster, people can search for family members, as long as they know the phone number or a complete address. Once you're registered, your parents will be able to find out that you survived."

I almost said, "That isn't necessary because I don't have any parents," but I caught myself. A statement like that would only call attention to me and probably bring Hiss to the scene. Instead, I gave my name as Kaitlyn Smith and made up a fake address and phone number. "I'll enter your information on the Red Cross website," she said. She handed me a folded blanket and a pillow.

"Pick out any empty cot you want and it will be your bed as long as you're here."

"I have my dog with me," I said. "Is it okay to bring him in?"

"No, it isn't."

"He'll stay on the floor by my cot. He won't bother anyone."

"I'm sorry. Animals are not allowed inside. Some people are allergic to them. He can be outside with you, as long as he's leashed."

"The leash was in my backpack, and it blew away in the tornado."

"You can't keep an unleashed dog on the premises," she told me. "There's too much risk that it would bite someone, or get in a fight with another animal."

"Do you have something I could use for a leash? A piece of rope, maybe?"

She looked down at the table, as if expecting a coil of rope to miraculously appear in front of us. Then she shook her head.

"Sorry."

"Thanks, anyway," I said, handing back the pillow and blanket. I turned to open the door.

"Where are you going?" she asked.

"I don't know, but I can't stay here without Snickers."

"If you can find a way to leash your dog, you can try keeping him here. As long as he's under control and nobody complains, I don't see what it would hurt." She smiled at me. "I have a dog myself," she added.

"Thanks. I'll look for something I can use as a leash."

I didn't want to leave the shelter. Snickers and I both needed a source of food, and some sleep. I'd slept little the night before and I felt a weariness deep in my bones. I knew Snickers needed rest, too, and I still hoped to find a veterinarian to examine the lump on his head. It made sense to stay here, at least for a day or so.

I asked the people who were distributing food if they had something I could use as a leash. "I can't stay at the shelter unless I find a way to tie my dog," I explained.

They looked around but found nothing suitable.

Then one of the women said, "You can have my belt, if you want it. That might work." She unbuckled her belt and slid it free from the loops of her jeans. It was a woven belt, so the tongue of the buckle would pierce through at any spot. I looped it around Snickers's neck and fastened it. The belt length that was left was a lot shorter than his real leash had been, but it worked to keep him beside me.

"Thank you," I told the woman. "I'll return it if I can find something else to use."

"Meanwhile, I hope my pants stay up," she said, and we both laughed.

I led Snickers back to the shelter building and this time I took him inside. I asked the woman at the table if she had tweezers, and she helped me get the splinter out from under my fingernail.

Then I picked up a blanket and pillow, claimed a cot, and lay down. Snickers did not want to lie on the floor beside me; he hopped up on the cot. Although it was crowded that way, I decided to let him stay. Once I fell asleep, my grasp on the belt would loosen and I wouldn't know if Snickers wandered off. If he was lying next to me, I would know if he moved. With me under the blanket and Snickers on top of it, I closed my eyes. Even with the low murmur of strangers talking, I fell asleep right away.

When I woke up, the room was crowded. Every cot was occupied, and so were the chairs. Some people sat on the floor. I took Snickers outside and walked him for a while, then returned and got in the food line, which now snaked around the corner of the building. When I got to the window, I was given a tuna sandwich, an apple, and a bottle of water. "Could I please have an extra sandwich?" I asked. The man inside handed it to me.

Most people took their food inside and sat on their

cots to eat, but I walked to the edge of the yard and sat in the grass. I didn't want to take a chance that some fussbudget would complain about me giving a sandwich to a dog. Tuna is not my favorite, but I ate it. Snickers gobbled his sandwich, including the lettuce. All of his months of scrounging for scraps had apparently made him an unfussy eater.

Back inside, I noticed that the walls were now covered with papers, photos, and other items that were attached with masking tape. People were walking around the room looking at them, as if they were in an art gallery.

Leading Snickers with the belt/leash, I circled the room, too. There was a graduation photo of a pretty young woman in a red cap and gown, with a gold tasseled cord draped around her neck. There were pictures of a black cat. A loop of bright blue beads hung from a pushpin that had been jammed into the wall. A page from a calendar, with notations on the dates, hung between a lace doily and a packet of pumpkin seeds. Most of the papers and photos were torn and dirty, and I realized these were things people had found and brought here, hoping the people they belonged to would reclaim them.

I remembered the drawing I had found. I took it out of my pocket, smoothed it open, pricked it with a pushpin, and stuck it on the wall. Maybe Suzy's parents were here; maybe they would be happy to find her drawing.

Two women walked around the room ahead of me. "I wouldn't mind losing my house so much," one of them said, "if I could still have the pictures of my grandparents, and of my kids when they were little."

A few minutes later the same woman said, "Oh! Here's Grandma and Grandpa!" She was standing in front of a long table that was piled with items that had been picked up. I saw her hug a small framed photo to her chest.

The table also contained a tattered blue baby blanket, a leather-bound Bible, and a teddy bear. Curious, I went closer.

When I reached the table, I stopped and stared in disbelief. A pink diaper bag sat at the edge of the table and there, partly hidden behind it, was my backpack! While I had slept, someone had brought my backpack to the shelter and left it on the table. With trembling hands, I opened it.

I took out my UCLA sweatshirt, my underwear, the bag of cashews, Snickers's bowl and biscuits, and, yes, my money. All of it. I clasped the backpack, holding it tightly as a wave of gratitude swept over me. Whoever had found my backpack could have removed the money before they brought it here. No one would ever have known. But they didn't take my money. They brought the backpack here and left it with the contents intact, hoping the owner would find it. And I did.

I took Snickers's leash out of my backpack and snapped it on his collar. Then I removed the belt and took it back to the woman in the food van.

"Thanks for the loan," I told her.

She smiled. "Anytime."

The backpack gave me fresh hope and determination. Nothing could stop me now. I had survived a tornado!

13

The next morning, as Snickers and I ate scrambled eggs and toast, with orange juice for me and dog biscuits for him, I saw Zooman and Hunker waiting in line for food. I wondered what they would do if they saw me. Probably they'd complain that Snickers was a vicious dog who had tried to attack them.

I turned my back to them and positioned myself between them and Snickers so they wouldn't notice him. He's definitely a one-of-a-kind dog; if they saw him, they'd recognize him.

A white van with green lettering on the side pulled in to the parking area, and a man with a large video camera got out. I heard him introduce himself as the reporter for a TV station. "We're doing a feature story on heroes of the tornado," he said.

Remembering what Jake had told me about the media wanting to find the girl who had helped Randy, I decided it was time to move on. Keeping my face turned away from Zooman and Hunker, I led Snickers inside and went back to our cot.

Many of the people who had slept at the shelter had already gone. Some had been picked up by friends or relatives; others had left on foot or had hitched a ride with a volunteer. Everyone was eager to return to their homes to survey the damage.

Although the food was tasty, and the cot comfortable enough, I knew I needed to leave before any questions were asked about where I lived, and before Zooman and Hunker caused trouble.

I folded my blanket and put my pillow on top of it. We had all been instructed to sign out when we left permanently so that anyone searching for us would know we weren't coming back to the shelter. I didn't need to do that. No one would come here looking for Kaitlyn Smith, or for Sunny Skyland.

I waited until the woman at the entry table was engaged in a conversation with someone else, then I added my blanket and pillow to a stack that was already started, and walked out the door. Zooman and Hunker were at the food station, receiving their breakfasts. I quickly went around to the back of the building, passed a chugging generator, and headed into town.

Snickers seemed to have recovered from his blow to the head. The lump was barely noticeable. Although he still walked as if his joints needed oiling, he apparently felt okay. I decided it wouldn't be necessary to find a veterinarian, after all. What I needed to find was transportation to Washington State.

An hour later I saw restaurants, motels, and other businesses ahead. As I neared the edge of town, lights suddenly came on in all the buildings.

While I waited at a traffic light, a taxi idled in the street beside me, giving me a new idea.

I waved for the cab to pull over. The driver, a man about Rita's age, looked as if he should do more walking and less driving. His cheeks were chubby and his ample stomach barely fit behind the steering wheel. His face had laugh lines, and he smiled as he said, "Where to, Miss?"

"How much would you charge to drive me to Washington?" I asked.

The smile turned to a scowl. "Don't play games, kid," he said as he looked over his left shoulder, preparing to pull away.

"Wait!" I cried. "I'm serious!"

Looking skeptical, he stayed at the curb. "Where do you want to go?" he asked.

"Enumclaw, Washington."

"Washington State?"

"Yes." I fished my map out of my backpack and offered it to him, but he didn't take it.

"I can't do that," he said. "I only work an eight-hour day. My back kills me if I drive longer than that."

"How much would it be if you drove me west for four hours, and then returned alone?"

"I'd have to charge you for both directions. I can't drive an empty cab for four hours."

That seemed reasonable. "How much?" I asked.

"How are you going to pay me?"

"Cash."

"Where did you get the money?"

"I didn't steal it, if that's what you're wondering, and I didn't sell drugs or do anything else illegal. I found the money and I advertised for the owner and nobody claimed it. It's mine, fair and square."

He thought for a few seconds. "Four hundred dollars," he said.

For eight hours, that came to fifty dollars an hour. I doubted he averaged fifty dollars an hour. If he did, lots more people would want to be cab drivers.

"How much do you make in a normal eight-hour day?" I asked. The taxi said CHARLEY'S CAB on the side, so I was pretty sure he owned the vehicle and didn't have to share what he got with a boss.

"Four hundred dollars," he said.

I didn't believe him. "I don't have that much," I said, figuring if he could lie, so could I. "I'll give you one hundred-fifty dollars."

"Two-fifty, paid in advance."

"Two hundred, half now and half in four hours."

I could tell he was tempted, so I added, "And I'll buy lunch."

He laughed. "You drive a hard bargain," he said. "Hop in."

As Snickers and I climbed into the backseat of Charley's cab, I looked at my watch. It was eleven o'clock. I wondered where we'd be in four hours.

"You're lucky I just started today," he said. "Otherwise I couldn't do this."

"Are you Charley?" I asked.

"At your service. And you are . . . ?"

"Brenda." I have no idea where that name came from since I've never known anyone named Brenda. It just jumped out of my mouth. So far on this trip, I'd been Sunny, Kaitlyn, and now Brenda. At least Snickers stayed the same.

Charley did not drive off. He seemed to be waiting for something. Finally I realized what it was. I opened my backpack, took out five of the twenty-dollar bills, and handed them to Charley. "Here's your down payment," I said.

One at a time he held each bill up to the light, checking to be sure it was not counterfeit.

"Thanks," he said, and pulled out into traffic.

I had never spent that much money at one time before. I hoped we'd go many, many miles in the four hours.

"Nice dog," Charley said. "What is he?"

"A mutt."

"Mutts are the best kind," Charley said.

"His name is Snickers." I almost added that we were taking a cab because the bus driver wouldn't let him on the bus, but I caught myself. I needed to be careful about how much information I divulged. I didn't know whether or not Rita had honored my request not to report me missing. Cops all over the country might be searching for me.

It dawned on me that even if Rita had reported me missing, nobody would be looking for a girl with a dog. Snickers was now part of my disguise.

"Good dog," I said as I patted his head. "Good Snickers."

Snickers put his head on my knee, heaved a sigh, and closed his eyes. I leaned my head on the back of the seat and closed my eyes, too. *I'm coming, Starr,* I thought. *I'm getting closer by the minute.*

A short time later I felt the cab stop. Looking out, I saw a sign that said WELCOME TO WYOMING. "You need to walk across the state line," Charley said. "You're a minor. I'm not certain, but I think I could get in trouble for driving you into a different state, even if you've asked me to do it."

I got out and walked past the sign while Charley pulled the cab ahead, into Wyoming. Then I climbed back in, we drove on, and I soon fell asleep.

I jerked awake when the cab stopped. We were parked at a highway rest area.

"Sorry to wake you," Charley said, "but this is the last rest area for a while."

I looked at my watch. Twelve-thirty. I had slept for more than an hour! "That's okay," I said. "I need to stretch."

While Charley was in the restroom, I snapped the leash on Snickers and led him to the dog-walk area. Then Charley held the leash while I took my turn in the restroom.

"I used to have a dog," Charley said as we pulled back onto the road. "A mutt named Freddie. He was a good dog."

"What happened to him?"

"He lives with my ex-wife. She got him when we divorced. We didn't have any kids, so we had a custody battle over the dog. She won."

"Do you ever see him?"

"No. She took him along when she moved back to Iowa, where she was from. I miss him a lot. More than I miss my ex-wife."

"Why don't you get another dog?" I asked.

"I will, someday. Right now I'm still missing Freddie."

I understood. A Hiss caseworker had once asked me why I was sad, and I told her I missed my friend Jessie. I'd left Jessie behind when I moved to a new foster home and I missed playing with her.

Using her cheerful kindergarten-teacher voice, Ms. Hiss had said, "You can make a new friend. Then you won't miss Jessie."

I had glared at her. A new friend would be nice, and I might make one, but that person wouldn't stop me from missing Jessie. The new friend would not know the secret code that Jessie and I had made up. She wouldn't call me Sunnysideup, or let me sleep with her stuffed elephant when I stayed at her house overnight. I felt like saying, "People are not interchangeable. If you lose one friend, you can't just substitute somebody else. It doesn't work that way."

I didn't say anything, though. If Ms. Hiss had to be told how friendship works, she wouldn't have understood what I was talking about.

———

The taxi approached a small town, and Charley asked if I was hungry. "There's a deli ahead," he said. "Might be a good time for some sandwiches."

We left Snickers in the cab while we went in, but we got our food to go so we could eat with him. Even with the windows rolled partway down, it was too warm to leave him in the vehicle. As promised, I paid for lunch.

I ordered a plain ham and cheese, no mayo, no oil and vinegar, for Snickers.

"Do you always feed your dog people food?" Charley asked.

"Only when we're traveling. It's easier than trying to carry dog food along."

Charley moved the cab to a shady spot, and we opened the doors while we ate.

I had just finished my sandwich when Charley asked, "Are you running away?"

"No," I said.

"I don't believe you," he said. "I'm not going to turn you in, if that's what you're thinking."

"Then why do you care?"

Charley shrugged. "I like you. You seem like a good kid, and you're nice to Snickers. People who are kind to animals can usually be trusted. I don't want to see you making a mistake."

"I'm going to see my sister," I said, then instantly regretted saying it.

"She lives in Enumclaw?"

"Look, Charley, I like you, too. It's real nice of you to take Snickers as a passenger and to drive so far knowing you'll just have to turn around and drive back by yourself. It's nice of you to worry about me, too, but I really don't want to get into a discussion about where I'm going. Okay?"

"Okay." He turned on the radio then and we listened to country western music and commercials while we drove on.

As it got close to three o'clock, when the four hours would be up, I watched out the window for a town. All I saw were acres and acres of empty fields, stretching as far as I could see. We were in the middle of ranch country, with no town in sight. It looked as if Snickers and I were going to walk a while today whether we wanted to or not. I was glad I'd bought a fresh bottle of water at the deli.

By 2:55, I began to get uneasy. It was isolated out here. What if some sleazebag came along and tried to get me to go with him? Would Snickers protect me again, or would he wag his tail as I was forced into Sleazebag's car? What if there was another tornado? Stop it, I told myself. Instead of imagining the worst possible scenario, try to think positive. Maybe Snickers and I could find a nice barn to sleep in overnight.

When the dashboard clock said 3:00, Charley pulled the cab onto the shoulder of the road and looked back at me. "Four hours are up," he said.

"Right."

Fences crowded the road on both sides. I didn't see a barn, or a farmer on a tractor, or even a silo or water tower in the distance.

I wanted to beg Charley to drive farther, but a deal's a deal and he had kept his end of the bargain. I snapped the leash on Snickers.

"Wait," Charley said. "I can't dump you off here, in the middle of nowhere. I'll drive you to the next town."

"What about your sore back?" I asked.

"I'll survive. I want to be sure you do, too."

"Thanks, Charley."

It was another fifteen minutes before we saw buildings. Calling it a town would be a stretch. There was a grain elevator by the railroad tracks, a ramshackle gas station, and a cluster of houses.

"Where do you want me to drop you?"

I didn't have much hope that a different bus driver would let me take Snickers along, but I didn't know what else to try. "The bus probably stops at the gas station," I said.

Charley pulled up to the gas pump and filled the tank. While he did that, I went inside. The gas station attendant, who wore bib overalls and no shirt, seemed surprised when I opened the door. I don't think he got a lot of customers.

"Does a bus stop here?" I asked. "Going west?"

He removed the toothpick from his mouth and said, "Yep."

"When does it come?"

He looked up at a big clock on the wall. "Usually goes through a little after six," he said.

"Goes through? It does stop here, doesn't it?"

"Yep. So long as you flag it down. Stand out there by the gas pump and when you see the bus coming, you wave your hands over your head so the driver knows to stop. Otherwise he don't bother."

I knew the routine, and hoped there were not any smart-aleck boys in this town.

I was sure I knew the answer to my next question, but I asked it anyway. "Do I buy a ticket first, or pay the driver?"

"You pay the driver."

I thanked him and went back outside. What was I going to do for almost three hours?

"The bus stops here," I told Charley.

He went inside to pay for his gas.

I walked Snickers to a sparse patch of grass and wondered what I would do if this bus driver refused to allow a dog on board.

14

When Charley returned, Snickers wagged his tail as if Charley had been gone all day. Charley leaned down and scratched Snickers behind both ears. As I watched, I had an idea.

"I have a favor to ask of you," I said. "A huge favor."

"Now, I hope you aren't going to tell me you don't have the other hundred bucks, because I would not be a happy man if you tried to cheat me."

"I have the money," I said. I quickly took five more twenty-dollar bills out of my backpack and handed them to Charley. This time he put them in his wallet without holding them up to the light first.

"So, what's the favor?"

"Would you keep Snickers for a few days? Once I get to my sister's house, I'll be able to come back and get him. That should only be a week or so, and I can pay you for his food."

"You want me to board your dog."

"I'd get there a lot faster if I was traveling alone, and I know you'd be good to Snickers."

"You could put him in a kennel."

I looked around the sorry excuse for a town. "What kennel?" I said. "Even if there was a boarding kennel, Snickers would be miserable. He'd think I had abandoned him. He needs a warm bed and somebody to pet him and play with him and take him for walks." I could feel the tears trying to leak out of my eyes, and I blinked to keep them from falling. "I'm afraid the bus driver won't let me take Snickers on board," I said. "The last driver wouldn't take him. We had to walk, and we were caught in a terrible tornado. Snickers already knows you, and likes you. He wouldn't be scared if he stayed with you." My bottom lip trembled, and I bit it, to make it stop.

"Where are your parents?" Charley asked.

"I never knew my dad. My mom was killed in an accident ten years ago, and so was my grandma."

"Who do you live with now?"

"I'd rather not say."

"Look, Brenda, if that's your name. If you are going to trust me with Snickers, who loves you and who is your loyal companion, then you should be able to trust me enough to tell me the truth."

I hesitated.

"I think you could use some help right now," Charley said, "and I don't mind giving it to you, but I can't do it unless I know exactly what's going on. You need to level with me."

"If I do, will you keep it to yourself? Not tell anyone?"

"I can't promise that without knowing what you're going to tell me."

I looked at the concern in Charley's eyes and thought what my options were.

I decided to take a chance.

"My name is Sunny Skyland," I said. "I was separated from my twin sister when our mom died, and I haven't seen or heard about her since. I've been in a string of foster homes; I don't know where Starr is, but I hope to find her soon."

"Why are you going to Enumclaw, if you don't know where she is?"

I showed him the photo, and what was written on

the back. I explained my plan to find the house and talk to the people who live there now, and maybe the neighbors.

"Where did you get the cash?" Charley asked.

"I found a bag of money, just like I said, and I tried to find the owner, but nobody claimed it, so I'm using the money to look for Starr."

"Does your foster family know about this, or did you run away?"

"I ran away. But I left a note so my foster mom would know I hadn't been abducted."

"Were the foster people mean to you?"

"Not this time. My current foster mom is actually the best one I've ever had. Rita lives by herself and she's smart and nice."

"Why didn't you ask her to help you find your sister?"

I stared at Charley. It had never occurred to me to ask Rita to help me. I was used to living with people who didn't care about me. I was used to keeping my dreams secret. I realized Rita would have helped me, if I'd asked her to.

"I thought it was something I had to do by myself."

"You could call her now."

I shook my head. "Rita would make me come home. Even if she was willing to help me find Starr, she'd want me to come home first. I've gone through a lot to make it this far. I want to go the rest of the way, and see if I can find Starr by myself."

We stood quietly for a moment while Charley thought about what I'd told him. "So, will you take care of Snickers for me?" I asked.

"On one condition."

"What's that?"

"You let me call this Rita and tell her you're okay."

"She'll trace the call. She'll send Hiss after me."

"Who?"

"The social workers who run the foster-care system. If Rita told them I'm gone, which she probably did, she'd have to let them know that she's heard from me. They'd be here instantly to drag me back and probably put me in a different foster home, or maybe even in juvenile detention."

"You like this Rita?"

"Yes. I like her a lot."

"Do you know how much she's probably worrying about you? She has no idea if you're okay or if you're lying in a ditch somewhere with a knife in your back."

I knew Charley was right. Rita was undoubtedly frantic with fear over my safety.

"I'll use a public phone to call my brother in Florida," Charley said. "Then I'll ask him to call Rita from a public phone down there. He'll do it, no questions asked. He won't say anything except that you're okay and you'll be in touch with her soon."

I felt guilty about making Rita worry after she'd been so good to me, and Charley's plan sounded foolproof. Rita would know I was okay, Hiss wouldn't find me, I'd get on the bus for sure, and Snickers would be safe.

"Deal," I said.

We shook hands. Charley wrote his name, address, and phone number on the back of the gas receipt and handed it to me. "Here's my card," he said, grinning. "Call me when you're ready to pick up your pal."

I put the paper in my backpack. Then I wrote Rita's name and number on a sheet of my notebook paper and gave it to him. I set the box of dog biscuits, the water dish, and the plastic bags on the floor of the cab. "Thanks, Charley," I said.

"Do you have enough money left?" he asked. "If you don't, I can lend you some, and you can pay me back later."

"I'm okay," I told him, "but thanks for offering."

I hugged Snickers. "Be a good dog," I told him. "Charley's going to feed you and take care of you until I can come back for you." Again, I blinked back tears. For years I had prided myself on being a tough kid who never cried. Now I was on the verge of bawling practically every other minute. Snickers gave my cheek a big slurp, and I lost it, letting my tears fall onto his fur. I felt Charley's hand, patting my shoulder.

"He'll be fine," Charley said. "I'll take good care of him."

I took a deep breath, and put Snickers in the cab.

"Good luck," Charley said. "If you get into trouble, call me."

I stood in the dirt beside the gas pump and watched the cab drive away. The last thing I glimpsed was Snickers's nose, pressed to the back window, watching me. I hoped I was doing the right thing. Although I missed Snickers already, I knew he'd be better off with Charley than he would be traveling with me.

Once again, I was by myself. *The story of my life*, I thought as I found a shady spot where I could wait for the bus.

15

Without Snickers by my side, the bus driver hardly looked at me. I waved, he stopped, I paid my fare—and the next afternoon I was in Auburn, Washington. A meal, a shower, a night in a motel, and then I boarded a Metro bus. This time when I got off, I was in Enumclaw. Was Starr here, too? For the first time since our mother's funeral, were my twin and I in the same town?

My first stop was a Welcome Center, where a friendly man asked if he could help me.

"I need a map of Enumclaw," I told him.

"We have two," he said. "Take one of each." He removed two maps from a holder and handed them to me.

"There's plenty of other information," he told me, nodding toward a rack of brochures for various attractions. "There's lots to do in this area."

I thanked him and hurried out the door. I went into a small café called The Hornet's Nest, ordered a soda, and studied the maps. I decided to start with what appeared to be the two main streets, Griffin and Cole. I'd walk down one and look for number 1041. If I found it, I'd compare the house with the one in my picture and either knock on the door or go a block over and see if there was a number 1041 there. How many 1041s could there be?

If I didn't find a 1041 on the main streets, I'd keep looking, one street at a time, until I found my house.

The adrenaline began pumping as I paid for my drink and went back outside. I was close now. I might find the right 1041 today. Maybe I would even find Starr today!

At the corner, I noticed a cardboard Garage Sale sign taped to a telephone pole. Half a block away, the front yard of one house contained card tables filled with household merchandise for sale. As my eyes swept the scene, I saw a bicycle at the edge of the sale. I hurried closer. A sticker on the handlebars said ten dollars. It was a plain blue bike with no extra gears, but I knew I could travel a whole lot faster on a bike than I could if I walked.

"Is that your best price?" I asked the woman who was running the sale.

"It's a good bike," she replied. "You can try it, if you want to."

I mounted the bike and rode it a short way down the street. When I returned, the woman said, "I'd take eight dollars for it."

"Sold." I paid her and pedaled away, watching the house numbers as I rode.

It took me only ten minutes to find a house numbered 1031. Thinking I was close, I rode slowly, but the next house was 1051. I rode to the next street, where the numbers jumped from 1031 to 1043. It seemed that every street had a 1031, but instead of progressing to 1041, they skipped up to higher numbers.

Many of the homes were ramblers. In the picture, my family stood in front of a two-story house, with steps leading to a front porch.

I continued to ride my bike around Enumclaw, going farther away from the downtown area.

It was mid-afternoon when I found a house numbered 1041. The numbers themselves were missing, but I could see the outline of where they had been, over the porch. As soon as I saw the house, I knew it was the right one. The redbrick chimney matched the photo. A large fir tree grew off to the side, in the area between the sidewalk and the house. The tree seemed familiar, like an acquaintance whose name I couldn't remember. The tree couldn't be seen in the picture, yet I was sure it had been there when the photo was taken.

The house needed paint, and the roof shingles were dotted with patches of green moss. Dandelions had gone to seed in the front lawn and the seeds had blown away, leaving behind empty stems.

As I looked at the house, I saw Starr and myself as we had been in the picture—two happy little girls posing with their grandma and her dog while their mom aimed the camera. We had played in this yard, and slept in this house. This very same house!

Even though it now needed some repair, I felt a deep fondness for the house where I had lived with Mama and Grandma and Starr. This had been my home.

Feeling as if I had traveled backward in time, I walked up the porch steps and knocked on the door. A woman opened it about an inch, leaving a chain in place.

"I'm looking for some people who used to live in this house," I said. "Their last name was Skyland."

"I don't know them."

"Have you lived here long?" I asked.

"That isn't any of your business."

"I'm sorry," I said. "I'm trying to find my sister. We used to live here. I have an old picture of us standing in this yard with our grandma."

The woman's eyes softened slightly. "We rent this house," she said. "I don't know who lived here before we did. You'd have to ask the owner."

"What's the owner's name?"

"I don't know that, either. We pay the rent to a property management company. Just a minute, I'll get their card." She handed a business card through the crack. I thanked her and walked down the steps, feeling discouraged. I wasn't likely to find someone at a big company who would help me. Privacy rules would probably prevent them from telling me the owner's name.

I went to the house next door and knocked, but nobody answered. Nobody answered at the house on the other side, either. I would have to come back in the evening, when people were more likely to be at home.

As I nudged the kickstand up with my foot, I saw movement at the window of the house across the street, and realized someone was watching me. I wheeled my bike over there and approached the door. Before I could ring the bell, the door opened. A white-haired woman in an orange and blue flowered muumuu said, "What are you selling?"

"I'm not selling anything." I held up my empty hands. "I'm looking for someone who used to live there," I said, pointing. "I wonder if you might know where she is."

"Who are you looking for?"

"Her last name was Skyland."

"She's gone. Loretta Skyland was killed in a car wreck years ago, and her daughter, too."

Chills ran up my arms. This woman had known my grandma and my mother. "Loretta was my grandma," I said. "My sister and I lived with her when we were little. So did my mom."

"You're one of the twins?" The woman's eyes widened. "You're one of Marie's girls?"

I swallowed the lump in my throat. "Yes. I'm Sunny."

The woman opened the door wider and waved me inside. "Come in," she said. "I'm Connie. I'll fix us some tea."

I followed her into the kitchen and watched while she filled an old kettle with water and put it on the stove. "Sunny," she said, as if trying to remember more about me. "Sunny. You're the one who went to live with Loretta's sister. What was her name?"

"Cora. My great-aunt, Cora."

"Cora! Yes, that's right. Cora. Is she still living?"

"I don't know. I didn't stay with her very long. She sent me to live with her son."

"Jerod? That no-good who caused her nothing but trouble from the day he was born? He took you?" She sounded genuinely shocked.

"He didn't keep me long, either."

"Well, that's no surprise. I can't imagine Jerod putting himself out for anyone, not even an orphaned cousin. Where did he send you?"

I didn't want to go through the whole long list of people I'd lived with, so I said, "I became a ward of the state. I've been in foster homes."

"Maybe you were better off that way. Jerod had a mean streak." Connie poured tea into two china teacups, placed them on matching saucers, and set them on the table.

I sat across from her. "Now I'm looking for my sister, Starr. I hoped someone here in the neighborhood would know where she went to live."

"You came to the right place," she said.

"You know where she is?"

"I don't know exactly where she is now, but I know who took her after the accident. It was the Andersons, Al and Becky Anderson. They used to live down the street, and they didn't have any children, and when Loretta's sister said she could take only one of you girls, Becky and Al offered to adopt the other one." Connie's head bobbed up and down as she spoke, as if confirming her own facts. "They were a nice young couple."

Knowing how many rules and regulations Hiss has about foster kids, I was amazed that Starr and I had apparently been placed in new homes without anyone ever notifying the authorities.

"You said the Andersons used to live in this neighborhood. Do you know where they went?"

"No. They moved not long after they took the girl," she said. "Becky said they needed a bigger yard, with room for a swing set."

"Did any of your current neighbors live here back then?" I asked. "Maybe someone else kept in touch with them."

"No. The street has changed a lot these past few years." She shook her head sadly. "Nobody stays put anymore. They move in, live here a year or two, and move on. Some of the houses are rentals, and they're all owned by the same company. I think the company's trying to buy the whole block so they can tear everything down and build condominiums." Connie sipped her tea. "It isn't like it used to be, when folks raised their family in one spot."

"Do you have a telephone directory that I could look at?" I asked. Anderson was a common last name, but maybe first names would be listed.

"You aren't going to make a long distance call, are you?" Connie asked. "My phone bill's too high as it is."

"I'm not going to call anyone," I said. "I only want to see if there's a listing for Al and Becky Anderson. Maybe they still live in Enumclaw, and I can find their address."

She handed me the directory, and I turned to the *A* section. Several Andersons were listed, but no Al and no Becky. However, there were two Andersons with the initial *A*. I copied down both addresses.

"If you want to call the Andersons, it's okay," Connie said. "As long as it's a local call."

I could tell she was curious as a cat to know if one of the names in the directory was the one I wanted.

"I think it will be better if I go in person," I said. "Thanks for the tea and for your help."

"You let me know if you find your twin," Connie said. "I always liked Loretta. She made the best banana bread."

———

I rode back to the main part of town to get something to eat. While I ate, I marked the addresses for the two A. Andersons on my map. One was only eight blocks away; the other was a couple of miles east of town.

I tried the closer house first. When I rang the bell, a chorus of barking dogs erupted. They yipped and yapped so loudly that I didn't hear the door click. A young man with purple spiked hair put his foot in the door to keep a pack of Chihuahuas from rushing out.

"Stay back!" he said. "No barking!" The dogs kept yapping.

The heavy silver chains around the man's neck clinked as he edged out the door. He kept it cracked open, and the dogs pressed their noses to the crack, sniffing and barking.

"I'm looking for Al and Becky Anderson," I said.

"Not here."

"Are you Mr. Anderson?"

"I am, but my name isn't Al. It's Aaron."

"Sorry to have bothered you," I said.

He used his foot to shove the dogs back so that he could go inside. The door closed, but the barking continued.

I rode to the other address, hoping I was not nearing a dead end in my search. If this was not the right Anderson, what would I do next? How would I find Starr?

As I pedaled along, the homes I passed became bigger. Most had three-car garages and large lots. The address, when I found it, was a big white house with green shutters. Window boxes bloomed with pink geraniums and the lush green lawn made me want to walk barefoot on it. It was the kind of house you see on the cover of a magazine. While I sat on my bike, looking at the house, a young boy rode by on a scooter.

"Hi," I said. "Do you live around here?"

He stopped. "I live on the corner."

"I'm looking for the Anderson family," I told him. "Do you know if this is where they live?"

"That's it," he said.

"Do they have any kids?"

"Nope. No kids."

I tried to swallow my disappointment. This wasn't the right Anderson, either.

"They have a teenager, though," the boy said. "She babysits me sometimes."

A teenager! My scalp tingled as I asked, "What's her name?"

"Starr."

I could barely breathe. This was Starr's home. I had found her! I felt like shouting to the skies, *I found her! I found my twin sister!* but I tried to stay calm. I didn't want this little kid to be the first to know who I was. I wanted Starr to be first.

The boy pushed off on his scooter, rode down the street, and turned into the driveway of the corner house.

Suddenly I was aware of how scruffy I looked. Maybe I should get cleaned up before I went to the door. I wanted Starr's first impression of me to be favorable. I sat on my bike and debated. One part of me wanted to rush to the door and another part of me didn't. I realized my hesitation had nothing to do with my appearance. I was frightened. I felt the way I had the one time I had been in a school play, just before I went on stage— nervous, afraid I'd make a mistake, scared the audience wouldn't like me.

I had dreamed of my reunion with Starr for so long. In my dreams, it was always the same. I told her my name, she gasped and flung her arms around me. We cried tears of joy and swore we would never again be separated. Never!

Starr won't care what I'm wearing, I told myself. *She'll be so glad to see me that nothing else will matter.* I got off my bike and started up the curved brick path that led to Starr's front door.

16

I approached the house slowly. A honeysuckle twined around a trellis near the door, and I paused to inhale the sweet scent. After imagining this moment for so many years, now that it was here I wanted to savor it. It was really happening at last; I was about to be reunited with Starr.

My heart beat faster as I rang the doorbell.

A girl my age opened it. My eyes swept over her, noting the similarities. She had the same oval face as I have, the same dimple in the left cheek. Her hair was the color mine had been until I dyed it. It was Starr!

I could barely speak over the lump in my throat. Finally I managed to whisper, "Hi, Starr. I'm Sunny."

She raised her eyebrows, looking quizzical. "Who?" she said.

"I'm Sunny," I repeated.

She still looked blank.

"Your twin sister."

"You have the wrong house," she replied. "I don't have a sister." She started to close the door.

"Wait!" I said. "You were born on April tenth, right? And your mom was killed in a car accident when you were three."

A voice from behind Starr said, "Who is it, honey?"

"You'd better come," she said. "It's some girl claiming she's my sister."

A blond woman wearing a blue sweatsuit appeared behind Starr. She gasped when she saw me. Even with my dark hair, I could tell she saw the resemblance.

"Are you Becky Anderson?" I asked.

"Yes."

"I'm Sunny Skyland," I said. "I'm Starr's twin sister."

"I told her she has the wrong address, that I don't have a sister," Starr said. "You tell her, Mom. Maybe she'll listen to you."

The woman said, "I'm Starr's mother. Her adoptive mother. Come in, Sunny. We need to talk."

Starr gaped as her mother held the door for me.

Mrs. Anderson sat in an overstuffed chair, and motioned for me to sit, too. I chose the sofa. Starr remained standing.

"As you can see," Mrs. Anderson said, "this is something of a shock to us."

"Mother!" Starr said. "Are you saying I do have a sister? I'm a twin?"

"Yes," Mrs. Anderson said. "When your mother was killed, you and Sunny were separated. We got you, and Sunny went to your grandmother's sister." She looked at me. "Isn't that right?"

"Yes," I said. "She didn't keep me, though."

"She didn't?" Mrs. Anderson seemed stunned by that news. "But she loved you! She loved both of you. She wept when she signed the document that allowed us to adopt Starr. She only did it because she knew she couldn't possibly cope with two young children."

"Why didn't you tell me?" Starr said. She looked furious. Instead of being thrilled to find me again, she was angry at her mother for having kept me a secret.

"Your dad and I did not intend to deceive you," Mrs. Anderson said. "At first we had planned to arrange visits so that you girls would remain close, but you never talked about your twin. You never wondered where Sunny was, or said you missed her. If you had asked about your sister we would have tried to contact her, but you never once mentioned Sunny. As the months went by, it seemed best for us not to bring up the subject, either. You were happy; you had adjusted well. You didn't seem to miss your family, or your old life. We were afraid if we talked about your past, about your mother and your grandma and your sister, it would only stir up your grief."

The words hurt terribly. During those times when I had cried myself to sleep every night, missing Starr, she had not even asked where I was.

Mrs. Anderson continued, "We never heard from your great-aunt Cora, so we assumed she had made the same decision about not keeping in touch. After your adoption was final, and your last name was the same as ours, we decided to let the past be forgotten."

Starr sank into a chair, looking shocked.

Mrs. Anderson turned to me. "If your great-aunt didn't keep you, Sunny, where have you been?" she asked. "Who raised you?"

"First I went to live with her son, but he abandoned me. Since then I've been in a series of foster homes."

Starr stared at me as if I'd said I'd been living on Mars.

"Oh, my," Mrs. Anderson said. "Oh, that's terrible! We wanted both of you. At the time, I said it didn't seem right to separate twins, but everyone felt you should stay with a blood relative, if possible, and Cora swore she wanted one of you but couldn't handle both of you." She stood suddenly and told Starr, "I need to call your father."

"By all means," Starr said. "Let's hear what Daddy's excuse is for not telling me the truth all these years."

Mrs. Anderson clamped her lips together, clearly stung by her daughter's words. Then, without replying, she went to the phone and dialed. "Al?" she said. "Can you come home? Starr's sister just showed up."

They talked briefly while I looked at Starr and she looked at the floor.

"He's on his way," Mrs. Anderson said, after she hung up. She returned to her chair. "You say you've been in foster care," she said to me. "Here in Enumclaw?"

"In Nebraska."

"Nebraska! You've been living in Nebraska?"

"Yes. Great-aunt Cora's son took me along when he moved there."

"Who brought you here?" She looked out the window, as if expecting to see a car waiting for me out front.

"I came alone. Mostly I took the bus. A cab driver helped me. I walked a lot."

"Your foster parents let you take off across the country all by yourself?"

I hesitated. Should I tell the truth? I didn't want to begin my new life with Starr by telling lies. "My foster mom didn't know I was going," I said. "She doesn't know about my sister."

"You ran away?" Starr said.

"I had to find you," I said. "All these years, I've thought about you every day. When I finally had enough money to travel, I knew I had to look for you."

"But how did you know where to look?" Mrs. Anderson asked. "Starr has our last name now, and we moved years ago."

I handed her the picture. "It says Enumclaw, Washington, on the back," I said, "and you can see a house number. I decided the best way to find Starr would be to come to Enumclaw and see if I could find the house that's in the picture, so that's what I did. I hoped some of the neighbors might remember Mama and Grandma and us. One neighbor did remember; she told me your name."

"I'll bet it was Mrs. Polson," Mrs. Anderson said. "Connie Polson lives across the street from where you girls used to live. She is a big snoop, always watching everyone in the neighborhood. She's lived in the same house for decades."

"That's right," I said. "Connie Polson told me you took Starr, and I found your address in the telephone directory."

"So some old woman knows I have a twin sister?" Starr stood and began pacing around the room. "She knew all this time, but I didn't! She's probably told half the town. Everyone knows my background except me!"

Before Mrs. Anderson could answer, a man in a business suit rushed in. He stopped when he saw me. "Hello, Sunny," he said. "I'm Al Anderson, Starr's dad."

I stood, and we shook hands. Then he wrapped his arms around me and gave me a hug.

"Except for the hair color," Mrs. Anderson said, "she's a mirror image of Starr."

"She is not!" Starr declared. "How can you say that? She doesn't look anything at all like me. We probably aren't even related. Where's the proof?"

"She has a picture of the two of you, with your grandmother," Mrs. Anderson pointed out.

"That doesn't prove anything. Anyone could find an old photograph and pretend it was their own. She's probably an imposter who wants to con you out of your money."

"Calm down, Starr," Mr. Anderson said.

I couldn't believe how angry Starr was. I understood why she felt deceived at not knowing about me, but she must realize the secret had been kept with the best of intentions. If anyone had a right to be angry, it was me. Here were the Andersons, who seemed like nice people, telling me that they had wanted to adopt me. Instead of living with She-Who and the Boss of the World, I could have been here, with Starr. All these years, I could have been loved.

What bothered me the most, though, was that Starr apparently did not remember me. How could she forget the experiences that I cherished?

"If you're my sister," Starr said, "prove it."

"Our grandma was Loretta Skyland," I said, "and our mother's name was Marie Skyland."

"You could learn that from public records, or from an old obituary notice," Starr said. "Tell us something that isn't available in print or online."

"We used to play house," I told her. "We had white

wicker doll buggies and we pretended that our dolls were twins, the same as we were."

"I remember those buggies!" Mrs. Anderson said. "Loretta used to let you push them around the neighborhood, while she sat on the porch and watched."

Starr's expression changed. I suspected she *did* remember pushing our dolls in the wicker buggies.

"Do you remember our song?" I asked. I sang, "Twinkie, Twinkie, little star."

"It's twinkle, twinkle," Starr said, "not Twinkie, Twinkie."

"Not in our version." I stared at her. "You don't remember eating Twinkies and watching the stars come out?"

"No."

"We were in lawn chairs in the backyard. I was in Grandma's lap and you were in Mama's. We had blankets tucked around us and I remember feeling snug and safe." Again, I thought I saw a flicker of remembrance in Starr's eyes.

"I ate my Twinkie," I said, "while Mama sang, *Twinkie, Twinkie, little star.*"

"I don't like Twinkies," Starr said. "They're too sweet."

"You don't remember any of it?" I asked.

"No, and I'm not convinced you do, either. Maybe you're making all this up."

I felt as if a dark shade had been pulled across the sky, blocking out the sun. Starr didn't remember me. She didn't remember the Twinkies, or the song, or playing together. She didn't remember having a sister. What's more, she didn't *want* to remember.

"How can you forget your twin sister?" I whispered.

"I was only three," Starr said.

"So was I."

17

I looked down, twisting my hands in my lap. This reunion was nothing like the one I had envisioned. "Maybe I ought to leave," I said.

"No!" said Mrs. Anderson. "Please don't go yet. We want to know all about you, and what's happened to you over the years."

"It doesn't sound as if you've had much stability," Mr. Anderson said. "Not the life you would have had if they had let us take you both. I wonder why Cora didn't call us if she couldn't keep you herself. She knew we wanted you."

"She probably still wanted Sunny to stay in her family,"

Mrs. Anderson said. "And she hadn't heard from us. Maybe we were wrong not to keep in touch."

"That's water over the dam," Mr. Anderson said. "The important thing now is to find out what red tape we need to cut in order for Sunny to stay here for a while."

"What?" Starr exploded. "You're inviting her to live with us? We don't even know her!"

"I can't think of a better way to get acquainted," Mr. Anderson said. "Sunny, could you stay with us for the summer? And then, come fall, we can all decide if you should stay permanently."

"I've already decided," Starr said.

No one asked what her decision was. We knew.

Mrs. Anderson said, "We should start by calling the foster mother. We must do that anyway, to let her know that Sunny is with us and that she's safe."

For the first time, calling Rita sounded like a good idea to me. I wanted to talk to her; I wanted to get her opinion about what I should do. "I'll call her," I said.

"I am going upstairs," Starr announced, and she stomped out of the room. Her mother followed her.

I dialed Rita's number. When she answered, I said, "Hi, Rita. It's Sunny."

"Sunny! Are you all right?"

"I'm fine. I'm sorry I worried you, but . . ."

"Worried me? Do you have any idea how scared I've been?" I heard Rita pause and could tell she was trying to get herself centered, as she called it. "Where are you?"

"I'm in Enumclaw, Washington."

"Washington! I thought you were in Florida. I got a call from someone telling me you were okay, and I had the call traced to Florida. What are you doing in Washington?"

"I found my twin sister."

There was a stunned silence. Then Rita said, "You never told me you have a sister."

"We were separated when we were three. I didn't know where she was until today."

"Have you seen her?"

"Yes. I'm at her house now."

"How's it going?" Leave it to Rita to cut right to the important part. It was as if she could tell from my voice that I was unhappy.

"Not exactly like I thought. Starr got adopted right after we were split up. Her parents want me to stay here with them for the summer."

"I see. Is that what you want to do?"

"I—I don't know. When I left, I thought I wanted to

be with Starr more than anything in the world, but now that I'm here, I'm not sure. We haven't had much time together yet. She—she doesn't remember me."

"Oh, Sunny, I'm so sorry."

"Yeah. Me, too."

"How did you get there? Where did you get enough money for such a trip?"

I told Rita about the bag of money I'd found and my efforts to locate the owner.

"Let me speak to one of Starr's parents," she said.

I held the receiver toward Mr. Anderson. "She wants to talk to you," I said.

The two adults spoke for a few minutes. I heard Mr. Anderson give Rita his phone number. Then he gave the phone back to me.

"I told him you could stay for a week," Rita said. "That's *if* you want to stay that long. Do you?"

Did I? I wasn't at all sure, but I'd gone through so much to get here, it seemed as if I should stay the week, no matter how unwelcoming Starr was. Once she got used to me, she'd probably warm up. "Yes," I said.

"Then I'll get you a plane ticket to come home next Thursday. Even if it turns out that you want to return and stay there longer, you'd still need to come back here first and go through the channels with the foster-care system."

"Okay," I said.

"Is this what you really want to do?" Rita asked. "You don't sound sure."

"If I leave now, I'll always think I should have stayed and tried to make it work."

"Call me if you want to come home sooner. Call any time, day or night," Rita said. "It's all right to call collect. I'll accept the charges."

"Thanks."

"You want to know how worried I've been?" Rita asked. "I ate a whole package of Oreo cookies! I bought them to have on hand in case you came home, and then it was typical stress eating; they were gone before I knew I had opened the package."

"I'm flattered," I said. I had never seen a cookie enter Rita's mouth. She had never bought cookies for me before.

"I'm trying to make you feel guilty, not flattered."

"Rita, there's one more thing," I said. "I have a dog now."

"A dog!"

"He's staying with a friend of mine and I need to make arrangements to pick him up."

"Where did you get a dog?"

"It's kind of a complicated story," I said. "I found Snickers in a restaurant parking lot, and he was homeless, the same as me, so—"

"You are not homeless," Rita interrupted. "You have a home here with me. You will always have a home here."

"I adopted Snickers," I said, "but the bus driver wouldn't let me take him on the bus so we had to walk and we got caught in a tornado and—"

Rita interrupted again. "A tornado! Were you outdoors in that awful tornado? I saw pictures of it on the news."

"Yes. I wasn't hurt, but Snickers got hit on the head and was unconscious. We stayed overnight at a Red Cross shelter and then I met Charley, who's a cab driver, and he drove me more than four hours, and then I asked him to keep Snickers until I could come for him. I need to go get Snickers as soon as I can."

"You are a girl of many surprises," Rita said. "Let me speak to Mr. Anderson again, please. Maybe he can get Snickers and take him to Enumclaw and then I'll make arrangements for Snickers to fly home on your flight."

I gave the phone to Mr. Anderson. He listened a minute and then said, "The dog can't stay here. Starr is afraid of dogs."

"Snickers is as gentle as a kitten!" I said. "He wouldn't hurt anyone and I'll take care of him. He won't be any trouble."

"If I go get the dog," Mr. Anderson told me, "we'll board him at a kennel until you leave. Where is this dog?"

I got out Charley's address and told him the name of the town. It turned out that Charley lived almost as close to Rita as he did to the Andersons, so in the end, Rita said she would go get Snickers herself. "It will give me something to do while I wait for you to come home," she said, "and the dog will be waiting when you get here."

After we finished talking to Rita, I called Charley.

"Hey!" he said. "Glad to hear from you. Did you find your sister?"

"Yes. I'm at her house now."

I told him the plan and asked if it was okay for Snickers to stay with him for a few more days, until Rita could pick him up.

"He can stay as long as he wants," Charley said. "I was kind of hoping you wouldn't come back for him so I could keep him."

"No chance," I said. "Thanks, Charley."

When I'd completed my call, Mr. Anderson said, "You're probably tired. Maybe you'd like to rest a bit before dinner."

As soon as he said it, I realized I was exhausted. Besides riding my bike for hours, this had been an emotional few days, especially this afternoon. My thoughts were still whirling like the tail of the tornado, and I longed to lie down and replay everything that had happened, to try to sort it out.

Mrs. Anderson came in. "We're going to give Sunny the den for now," she said.

"What about Starr's room? She has twin beds," Mr. Anderson said. "No pun intended."

"I think Sunny needs some privacy," Mrs. Anderson said. What she probably meant was, Starr will throw a fit if we make her share her room, even with her twin sister.

"The den will be great," I said.

"Do you have luggage?" Mr. Anderson asked.

"Just my backpack. I left my bike out in front."

"Let's put it in the garage, where it's safe," he said. I followed him to the garage and watched while he pushed a button that made one of the garage doors open. I got my bike and wheeled it in beside a new Prius.

———

"You're going to need more clothes," Mrs. Anderson said as she led me to the den. "Tomorrow we'll go shopping. Starr loves to shop. Do you?"

"Yes," I said, although the only time anyone had ever taken me shopping was when Rita bought me new clothes when I first went to live with her. We'd had a great time that day. She let me try on anything I wanted, and then I'd step out of the dressing room to show her how I looked and we'd decide if we liked the item or not.

It wasn't only the new clothes that made this a happy memory; it was the feeling I'd had that someone cared about me and wanted me to look good. I realized Rita had given me more than jeans and tops that day; she had given me love.

Her words came back to me: *You'll always have a home here.* I realized how foolish I'd been to assume that once I found Starr, I'd instantly have a permanent home. I'd had a simplistic dream for a complicated situation.

Mrs. Anderson opened a hide-a-bed that was already made up with sheets and a blanket. "For now, you can sleep here," she said. "There's a bathroom across the hall. Let me know if you need anything."

"Thanks," I said.

"I'm glad you're here, Sunny," she said. "Starr will be glad, too, once she gets used to the idea. She's really a wonderful girl."

"I should have called first, instead of just show-ing up."

"It doesn't matter. You rest now, and we'll talk later."

I went across to the bathroom and took a long shower and shampooed my hair. According to the information that had come in the box of dye, it would take twenty-eight shampoos before my hair returned to its natural color. However, I had not left the dye on the full amount of time, so it was already beginning to fade, and I wanted to hurry that process along. I knew the resemblance to Starr would be greater if our hair was the same color.

I lay on the bed, trying to put myself in Starr's place. How would I feel if a stranger appeared with no warn-ing and claimed to be my twin sister? I'd probably feel apprehensive, too, if I had no memory of a sister, but I didn't think I'd be as negative as Starr was. I would be curious. Whether I liked the idea or not, I'd want to know who my sister was and what her life had been like since we were separated.

———

Dinner that night was strained. Mr. and Mrs. Ander-son tried to ignite the conversation, but I felt ill at ease.

Starr gave only one-syllable answers to questions and appeared not to listen when I talked.

"Starr is a poet," Mr. Anderson told me. "She's been writing poetry for years. Do you write poetry, Sunny?"

"No," I said. "I love to read it, though. I used to read only novels, but Rita likes poetry and she got me started on that." I turned to Starr. "I'd like to read some of your poems."

When Starr didn't respond, Mr. Anderson said, "You'll be impressed. Starr has a lot of talent."

I took a bite of my baked potato.

"Tell us about Rita," Mrs. Anderson said.

"She's single," I said. "She works at home most of the time, editing a business journal. One day a week she teaches yoga classes."

"How long have you been with her?"

"Five months." It seemed longer than that. In some ways, I felt as if I'd known Rita for many years.

"So you don't have a long-term relationship," Mr. Anderson said. "She probably wouldn't fight to keep you."

I put down my fork and looked at him, surprised. Was he saying they wanted me to live with them permanently? Starr looked horrified, and I knew she was wondering the same thing.

"Rita lets me make my own decisions," I said.

18

While we ate brownies for dessert, Mrs. Anderson said, "What shall we do tomorrow? Do you girls want to pack a picnic and go up to see the wildflowers? They should be in full bloom at this time of year."

"I'm going swimming with Abby tomorrow," Starr said.

"Do you have a swimsuit with you, Sunny?" Mrs. Anderson asked.

"No."

"We'll buy you one, first thing tomorrow. We can see the wildflowers another day."

"Mother," Starr said, "Abby invited me to go swimming at her club. I can't just bring along an extra person."

"Of course you can. If you call Abby and tell her that your twin sister is here, I'm sure she'll be eager to meet Sunny."

"No," I said. "It's okay. Starr, you go ahead with your plans. I'll be fine. Really."

"Then the two of us will go shopping," Mrs. Anderson declared.

And that's what we did. While Starr was off swimming with her friend, Mrs. Anderson took me to a dozen stores. It was almost like shopping with Rita. Almost. The differences were that Mrs. Anderson never looked at the price tags, and she didn't make me feel special, the way Rita had. I got the feeling Mrs. Anderson wanted me to be well dressed so as not to reflect poorly on Starr.

I felt ashamed for having such thoughts when Mrs. Anderson was being so nice to me. I pushed them aside and promised myself I'd make every effort to be friendly to Starr, no matter how much of a brat she was.

By the end of the afternoon, I had two new pairs of jeans, a pair of shorts, three tops, a sweater, some socks and underwear, new sandals, and a pink duffel bag that was the right size to fit in the overhead luggage space on my flight home. She also took me to a bookstore and let me choose a couple of new novels.

"Thank you," I told Mrs. Anderson. "I love everything you got for me."

"I hope this is only the first of many shopping trips," she replied. "Next time, Starr can come with us. Even though you and Starr are fraternal twins rather than identical twins, you have the same sweet personality." I didn't know what to say to that, so I said nothing.

When we got home from shopping, there was a voice-mail message from Starr saying she'd been invited to stay at Abby's for dinner and would be home around eight. Mrs. Anderson looked angry when she listened to the message, but she didn't call Starr and tell her she had to come home.

Mr. Anderson arrived home from work shortly after we returned from shopping. "I thought I'd take my girls out to dinner, to celebrate being together," he said.

"Starr is eating at Abby's house," Mrs. Anderson said.

His eyes narrowed briefly before he said, "Do you like Mexican food, Sunny?"

"It's my favorite."

"Then that's what we'll do."

We had a delicious dinner at a Mexican restaurant and then they showed me the town's public art. There was a huge loggers memorial sculpture that showed a pair of oxen pulling a downed tree while a logger urged them on. "Logging was an important industry here for many years," Mr. Anderson explained.

They showed me two other sculptures. My favorite was a bronze colt that stood on a street corner in the downtown area. I had seen it when I went to the visitor's center, but I enjoyed seeing it again.

After the tour, we went home and had ice cream. We had just finished when Starr arrived. "There's still plenty of ice cream," Mrs. Anderson said.

"No, thanks. I had dessert at Abby's house."

"Sunny and I had a good shopping trip," Mrs. Anderson said. "Would you like to see what we bought?"

"I'm really tired," Starr said. "I'm going to bed early."

Mr. Anderson opened his mouth as if he wanted to object but then said nothing. I got the feeling Starr's parents had decided not to push her to be nice to me but instead were hoping she'd come around by herself.

After Starr went upstairs, I excused myself and went into the den. I heard the TV go on, and Mr. and Mrs. Anderson talking together in the living room. I went quietly up the stairs and tapped on Starr's bedroom door.

"Who is it?"

"It's Sunny. Can I talk to you for a minute?"

"About what?"

"Nothing special."

"Oh, I suppose so. Come on in."

I went in. Starr was sitting on the bed, propped up with pillows. I sat on a small upholstered chair.

"I know you're unhappy that I'm here," I said, "and I'm sorry about that. I thought you would have the same memories that I have. I never dreamed that you wouldn't remember me."

"You could at least have written first, or called. It's a shock to find out I have a twin sister and nobody bothered to tell me about her."

"I know. I assumed you knew about me."

"Well, I didn't."

"You really don't remember me at all?"

"I vaguely remember playing with someone. I thought it was a friend."

"I'm not going to stay all summer, if that's what you're worried about," I said. "I'll be here only until Thursday. When I get back to Rita's, I plan to stay there."

"Mom is trying to bribe you," she said. "Buying all

those clothes for you is supposed to make you want to stay longer."

"I don't think that's true. Your mom was only being nice. She wanted me to have enough to wear during my visit."

"Think what you like," Starr said, "but I know her better than you do."

"I just—I just want to say that I'd really like to get to know you better. I mean, how often do you get a chance to meet a twin sister? It'll probably be years before we see each other again."

"If ever."

"If ever," I agreed. "So let's be friends for these few days."

Starr didn't respond.

"Are you afraid of me?" I asked.

"Afraid? Why would I be afraid?"

"I don't know. You act as if you fear something bad will happen if you get to know me."

"You're crazy. I'm just not thrilled to have my life disrupted by someone I don't know who moves in and wants to instantly become best buddies."

"Okay," I said as I stood. "I get the message."

I went back to the den and sat on the edge of the bed. Thursday seemed a long way off.

The old song ran through my mind, but this time I changed one word: "Twinkie, Twinkie, little Starr. How I wonder *who* you are." For ten years, I had wondered where my sister was. Now that I had found her, I realized I didn't know *who* she was. I had searched for a girl who existed only in my mind.

I picked up one of my new books, hoping it would be the kind of story where I'd forget about my regular life and become totally engrossed in the lives of the characters.

I had just finished Chapter One when Starr screamed. The first scream was followed immediately by another, even more shrill. I dropped my book and rushed to the den door.

Starr was at the top of the stairs, jumping up and down as if her shoes were on fire. Mr. and Mrs. Anderson came running from the living room and looked up at her.

"What's wrong?" Mrs. Anderson asked.

"What happened?" Mr. Anderson said.

Starr was waving a sheet of paper over her head. "I won!" she shouted. "I won! I won! I won!"

"Won what?" her dad asked.

Starr stopped jumping and bolted down the stairs. "I won the district poetry contest!" she yelled. "I'm going on to compete in the regionals!"

"Oh, Starr!" Mrs. Anderson said. "That's wonderful! I'm so proud of you!"

Starr handed the piece of paper to her dad. "They sent me an e-mail," she said. She grabbed the paper back and read it aloud: "Dear Ms. Anderson: I am pleased to inform you that your poem, 'Lilacs in Summer,' has won first place in the District Poetry Competition. It will automatically advance to the regional contest. That judging will take place in two weeks, and the winner there will go on to the State Poetry Competition.

"Congratulations on your winning entry. Attached is an affidavit for you to sign and return, stating that your poem is your own original work. This affidavit is required by the regional judges, so please return it as soon as possible."

Starr handed the paper to her dad again.

"I knew you would win," Mrs. Anderson said. "It's a lovely poem."

"Congratulations, Starr," I said.

"I told you she had talent," Mr. Anderson said. He was beaming with pride. "We need to call your grandparents."

"It's eleven o'clock in Chicago," Mrs. Anderson said. "They'll probably be in bed."

"For news like this, they won't mind being awakened."

I listened as he told his parents of his daughter's accomplishment. Then Starr got on the line and accepted congratulations. I kept waiting for them to mention me, but nobody did. Did the grandparents already know I was there or had my arrival not been newsworthy enough to merit a call?

When the call ended, Mr. Anderson said, "Do you have extra copies of your poem?"

"No, but I have it on my computer."

"Let's print a few. Grandpa asked me to mail one to him."

The three of them went up to Starr's room, talking about who else they needed to tell. "I'll notify the *Courier-Herald* tomorrow," Mrs. Anderson said. "They'll want to send a reporter out, and a photographer."

I returned to the den and picked up my novel. I thought about how many times in my life a good book had offered me a way out of a problem situation. From the time I had learned to read, whenever I was placed in a new foster home I got myself a library card as soon as I could. I tried to always have at least two unread books so that if I needed to escape my real life, I had other, fictional lives waiting for me. Books had taught me new ideas and had shown me ways of life that I would not have known about otherwise, and they offered a refuge when, like now, real life seemed too hard.

I was glad Starr's poem had won. I was happy to see Mr. and Mrs. Anderson's pride in their daughter. But I wasn't a part of their celebration, or their family. My dream of a permanent home with Starr had been a foolish fantasy.

I picked up my book and began to read.

19

When I went to the kitchen for breakfast the next morning, I saw that Starr's poem was taped to the front of the refrigerator. While I waited for my toast to pop up, I read it. Then I read it a second time. It was a good poem—an excellent poem—but Starr had not written it. I had read it before!

I tried to remember where I had seen it. A magazine? An English textbook? Surely Starr wouldn't be so stupid that she would copy a poem from one of her classroom books and enter it in a contest. She must have taken it from some out-of-print book or other source that she thought nobody would remember or find.

Rita had lots of poetry books and I sometimes browsed through them during the commercials when I was watching television. That's probably where I'd seen "Lilacs in Summer."

I debated what to do. If I said anything to Starr without proof, I was sure she would deny that she had copied the poem. If she was willing to sign an affidavit, swearing that it was her own original work, she wasn't likely to back down on my say-so, and the Andersons would take her side against me.

I found a sheet of paper and copied the poem, word for word. I had just finished when Mrs. Anderson came in. I folded the paper and put it in my pocket.

"I'm wondering if you and Starr would like to go into Seattle today," she said. "We could go to the Pike Place Market or walk along the waterfront."

Before I could answer, Starr came into the kitchen. "Count me out," she said. "Angie and Sarah and I are going to work on our routine for cheerleader tryouts."

"They could go with us," Mrs. Anderson said. "We'll take the van. There'll be plenty of time to practice cheerleading after Sunny leaves."

"I really need to go to the library today," I said. "I thought I'd ride my bike there." I felt sorry for Mrs. Anderson. She was trying so hard to plan fun outings that would create bonding between sisters, and everyone except her knew it wasn't going to happen.

"I can drive you to the library," Mrs. Anderson said.

"That's okay. I need the exercise and I'm not sure how long it will take me. I'm working on a project."

I could tell Mrs. Anderson was disappointed, and Starr was relieved. I wondered what she had told her friends about me. Maybe she had not told them anything. I knew she was counting the days until I left. Well, so was I.

The library didn't open until eleven, but I went early and walked around a while, wondering if I was doing the right thing. Maybe I should not try to find the published poem. Maybe I should just stay out of it and let Starr fool everyone. Of course, even if I didn't speak up, she might not get away with her deception. There was always a chance that someone else would recognize the poem. The judges in competitions of this kind must read lots of poetry. If I knew immediately that I'd seen it before, the odds were good that someone else would recognize it, too.

When the library opened, I went to the computer section, signed up for fifteen minutes online, and did a Google search for "Poem: Lilacs in Summer." Almost instantly, I got several responses and the second one I clicked was what I was looking for. It showed the whole poem and the author's name. "Lilacs in Summer" by Lois M. Kringdell. It had been published in 1896.

I got out the poem I'd copied and compared the two. Starr had not changed a single word. She had made no attempt to make the poem her own but had simply used it, word for word.

I printed out two copies.

Since I still had time left on the computer, I decided to check my e-mail to see if there had been any late responses to my ad. When I opened the in-box, there was a message from Rita, dated last Friday, the day I left.

> Dear Sunny,
> Please, please call me. I don't know what
> happened to make you leave, but whatever it
> was, we can fix it. I miss you like crazy and I'm
> scared that something bad will happen to you.
> I had hoped you would stay with me perma-
> nently, but if you want to live somewhere else,
> I'll help you do that as long as you are safe.
> Please come home! Love always, Rita

I logged off, then went to the magazine section, picked out some current issues, and found a soft chair. I was in no hurry to return to the Andersons' house. For one thing, I knew Starr and her friends would not want me there, and who wants to show up when they aren't welcome?

Also, I wasn't yet sure what to do about the poem. I could imagine how Starr's parents would react if I showed the published poem to them. They had welcomed me warmly and I didn't want to make them unhappy, no matter how much Starr deserved to get caught.

I tried to read one of the magazines but finally gave up. I sat in the library, staring at the shelves and wishing I had never found my sister. If I had not come, I could have kept my happy memories all of my life. I would always have thought that somewhere I had a wonderful twin who was exactly like me and who longed for me as much as I yearned for her.

Now I was stuck with reality. My twin sister not only did not remember me, she didn't want to know me at all. The fact was, I didn't like Starr. She was spoiled and self-centered and dishonest. When I left here to go home, I knew I'd never again make any effort to contact her.

Home. I smiled, thinking of Rita. While I had been traveling all those miles, I'd thought I was coming to find my family. It turned out I'd left my real family behind.

I put the magazines back. I asked the librarian if there was a public telephone that I could use and she told me where to find one.

I made a collect call to Rita, hoping she had not already left this morning to go pick up Snickers. I had her cell phone number, too, but she never answered when she was driving because she said it wasn't safe to talk and drive at the same time.

Please, I thought. *Please, please answer the phone!*

She did.

"I want to come home right away," I told her. "That way we could go together to get Snickers. It would be a lot easier for you to manage a dog in the car if I was there, too."

"I was planning to leave tomorrow," she said, "but Charley was flexible. He seems really fond of your dog." She paused, then added, "I don't think Snickers is the only reason you want to come back early. Things aren't going well?"

"My sister is a total jerk," I said. "We have nothing in common, and she doesn't want to get to know me."

"Her loss," said Rita.

"Mrs. Anderson keeps suggesting fun things for us to do together, but Starr always has an excuse. And you won't believe what I found out about her. She copied a poem and pretended she wrote it, and entered it in a contest and she won."

"Are you sure she copied it?"

"I'm at the library. I just found it online."

"Have you told the Andersons you want to leave?"

"No. I'm calling from a public phone."

"I'll see what I can do about an earlier flight," Rita said. "You'll need to go back to the Andersons' house so I can reach you to tell you the plans."

I started to cry. I couldn't help it. I was so relieved at the thought of not staying with Starr for another five days. "Thanks, Rita," I said. "I'm sorry I ran off without talking to you about Starr. It was a stupid move."

"Hey, we all make mistakes," she told me. "I'm just glad you're coming home. And your little dog, too."

I laughed. "He isn't so little," I said.

"I was afraid of that."

When I got back to the Andersons' house, Mr. and Mrs. Anderson were playing gin rummy.

"Starr and her friends went to a movie," Mr. Anderson said. "I can drive you to the theater, if you want. I'm sure you'd be able to find them. Sarah's mother is driving them home."

"No, thanks. I need to talk to you." I drank some water, took a deep breath, and said, "You've both been wonderful to me and I can't thank you enough for making me feel welcome here. But I realize now that I should have given you some warning. It was hard for Starr to have me just appear when she didn't even know I existed."

"It was a shock," Mrs. Anderson said.

"I called Rita from the library," I told them, "and asked her to see if she can get me on an earlier flight. I'd like to leave as soon as I can. That way I can go with her to pick up Snickers."

Even though they both said they wanted me to stay the full week, I could tell they thought it was a good idea for me to leave.

Ten minutes later, Rita called. Mr. Anderson answered. I heard him say, "Yes, I can take her to the airport. That will work out." Then he handed me the phone.

"Hey, Sunny," Rita said. "How'd you like to take the red-eye special tonight? It leaves Seattle at ten. You'd better say yes, because I already changed your ticket and it cost me a hundred-dollar transfer fee."

"Yes," I said.

After I hung up, the Andersons seemed at a loss for words.

"I need to pack," I said, and I headed for the den.

I folded my clothes and put them in the new duffel bag. It didn't take long. When I carried it out and set it by the front door, Mr. Anderson said, "I'm sorry this has not been a happier visit for you. I want you to know that if you ever need anything, anything at all, you can call us."

"Thank you," I said, although I knew I would not be calling.

"You could come back," Mrs. Anderson suggested, "after Starr's had time to adjust. We wanted to adopt you years ago, and we'd still like to explore that possibility."

"Starr's very lucky to have you for her parents," I said.

"We won't need to leave for the airport until seven tonight," Mr. Anderson said. "Would you like to go out for a Mexican dinner?"

"I want to talk to Starr alone," I said. "There's something I need to tell her."

"Maybe we'll send out for a pizza then," Mrs. Anderson said. "We'll eat at home, and then you girls can have plenty of time to chat."

"As soon as I've talked to Starr," I said, "I'd like to leave. I can get something to eat at the airport while I wait for my flight."

They looked surprised but didn't argue.

The remainder of the afternoon dragged. The Andersons quit playing cards and went outside to do yard work. I tried to read my book, but mostly I wandered around aimlessly.

Starr called at four to say she was at Sarah's house and had been invited to stay for dinner.

"No," her dad told her. "You need to come home. Sunny is leaving tonight and she wants to see you before she goes."

I could tell Starr argued with him, but for once she did not get her way. "I'll pick you up in ten minutes," Mr. Anderson said. He hung up, got in his car, and drove off.

When Starr arrived, she gave me a scathing look and said, "So, here I am. What do you want to talk about?"

"I need to see you alone," I said. "Let's go up to your room."

She led the way. She sat on her bed and glared at me.

I reached in my pocket and took out the copy of the poem, the one I'd printed at the library that included the author's name and the date the poem had been published. I handed it to her and watched as she read it.

Her face turned pale. "Where did you get this?" she whispered.

"As soon as I read 'Lilacs in Summer,' I knew you hadn't written it," I told her. "I'd seen it before. I wasn't sure where I'd read it, but I knew you weren't the author. I didn't want to use the computer here because I didn't know how long it would take me to find the poem and I didn't want to be interrupted, so I went to the library. I Googled the title and it popped up instantly."

Her hands were shaking so much, the paper rattled. She laid it on the bed.

"Are you going to show this to my parents?" she asked.

"No."

"Oh, I get it. This is blackmail. You keep quiet about the poem and, in return, I pretend it's okay with me for you to live here."

"I ought to be insulted," I said, "but instead I feel sorry for you."

"You feel sorry for me? That's a joke! You're the kid nobody wants."

"Not anymore. Rita wants me, and your parents want to consider adopting me."

"You're lying!"

"Ask them."

"They wouldn't adopt you unless I agreed to it, and I'll never do that."

"It doesn't matter," I said. "I wouldn't agree to it, either."

"What?"

"You heard me. I don't want your parents to adopt me. I like them a lot, but I want to live with Rita and Snickers."

"You're crazy. You'd choose a foster home and a flea-bag mutt over the chance to live here?" She waved one hand around. "What about the clothes and the big allowance?"

"Not important. Rita and I are going to take tennis lessons, and there's a trail where I can walk Snickers. I'm happy there."

Starr was quiet for a moment. Then she said, "You really aren't going to tell my parents about the poem?"

"No, but I think you should tell them."

She shook her head. "I can't. You don't know what it's like to have parents who think you're perfect. All my life they've expected me to be better than I am, to accomplish more than I'm capable of. No matter what I do, they always want more."

This is a problem? I thought. Nobody ever expected me to succeed at anything. Then I corrected myself: until Rita. Rita believes in me.

"They seem very proud of you," I said.

"They're proud of who they want me to be, not who I am." Tears dribbled down Starr's cheeks. "You were right when you guessed that I was afraid of you," she said. "I didn't want you to stay because I was afraid you'd be smarter than I am and do better in school and in sports. I couldn't stand the thought of competing with a twin and coming out second."

"You're taking a terrible chance by sending that poem and the affidavit to the regional contest," I said. "What if one of the judges recognizes the poem? You'll be publicly humiliated. Think what that would do to your parents. It would be a lot easier if you admitted what you did now instead of getting caught later."

"I'll withdraw the poem," she said. "I'll tell the judges I sent it by mistake. That way, Mom and Dad won't have to know. They'll just think I didn't win."

I looked at my sister. Even now that her plagiarism had been found out, she wasn't willing to take responsibility for what she had done. *Twinkle, Twinkle, little Starr. How I wonder who you are.* I didn't know the girl who sat in front of me. I no longer wanted to know her.

"Thanks for not telling on me," she said.

"Good-bye, Starr," I said.

20

Rita was waiting at the baggage claim, as we had agreed. I spotted her as I rode down the escalator.

She opened her arms and I rushed to hug her. Then she held me at arm's length and said, "What did you do to your hair?"

"As soon as I shampoo it twenty-two more times, it'll be back to my natural color."

The drive home took nearly two hours, and we never stopped talking. Rita told me she had notified the police about the bag of money I'd found.

"Did they know who it belongs to?" I asked. "Do I

have to give it back?" I hadn't thought about telling the police.

"Nobody had reported the loss and the amount didn't match any robbery, so it's yours to keep."

"Good, because I spent most of it getting to Starr's house."

"I'm in a peck of trouble with Hiss," Rita said.

"You told them I was gone?"

"Well, of course I did. I had to try to find you."

"Are they going to let me stay with you?"

"Yes. When they found out that you had voluntarily called and asked to come back, they agreed that we could try again. We're on probation for six months, though. If you leave again, they'll . . ."

"I'm not leaving again," I said. "Where would I go?"

"Who knows? Maybe you are one of triplets and there's a brother somewhere that I don't know about and one day you'll take off, looking for him."

"I don't blame you for being mad at me."

"I'm not mad at you, but I'm disappointed that you didn't feel you could tell me the truth. I would have helped you find your sister. I would have taken you to meet her."

"I know. I wish I'd done that, and I'm glad you're willing to give me another chance."

"I figured if I let you come home, I'd get Snickers, too," Rita said. "Ever since I arranged to work from home, I've wanted to have a dog."

"You're going to love him," I said.

"I'm sure I will."

"I thought my search for Starr would have a perfect, fairy-tale ending and we'd live happily ever after."

"You pursued your dream," Rita said. "It didn't turn out the way you had hoped, but now you can go on to other dreams."

"Is it too late for us to do the tennis lessons?"

"No. We can still do them."

"I'm going to write about my trip to find Starr," I told Rita, "and turn it in this fall for extra credit."

"That's a fabulous idea," Rita said.

"I thought about it on the plane," I said. "It might be too long for an essay. I might have to write a whole book."

Rita looked shocked.

"I already know the title and how it starts," I said. "I'm going to begin by saying my life was transformed by a craving for Twinkies."

"Twinkies?" Rita looked repulsed. "What do Twinkies have to do with searching for your sister?"

"You'll see when you read my book. I'm going to call it *Runaway Twin*."

"Good title," said Rita. "I can't wait to read it."

When we got to Rita's house, she said, "I have a welcome-home present for you." She handed me a bagel bracelet. "I used yellow yarn," she said. "For Sunny."

The bracelet was covered with buttons shaped like rainbows and little suns. I slipped the bracelet on my wrist. "Thanks, Rita," I said. "Thanks for everything."

"We'd better get to bed," Rita said. "I told your pal, Charley, that we'll be there tomorrow evening."

I walked into my room. My room. I looked around at the desk and the bed with its purple spread, and the Lava lamp. Then I noticed a new addition to my decor: a large dog bed with a cedar-filled pad sat next to my desk.

I'm home, I thought. *At last, I'm really home.*